45

pounds
(more or less)

45 pounds

(more or less)

K. A. BARSON

VIKING

An Imprint of Penguin Group (USA) Inc.

VIKING
An Imprint of Penguin Young Readers Group
Published by the Penguin Group
Penguin Group (USA) Inc.
375 Hudson Street
New York, New York 10014, U.S.A.

USA / Canada / UK / Ireland / Australia / New Zealand / India / South Africa / China
Penguin Books Ltd, Registered Offices: 80 Strand, London WC2R 0RL, England

For more information about the Penguin Group visit www.penguin.com

First published in the United States of America by Viking,
an imprint of Penguin Young Readers Group, 2013

LIBRARY OF CONGRESS CATALOGING-IN-PUBLICATION DATA IS AVAILABLE
ISBN: 978-0-670-78482-0

Printed in U.S.A.

1   3   5   7   9   10   8   6   4   2

Set in Napoleone Slab ITC Std   Designed by Kate Renner

ALWAYS LEARNING   PEARSON

FOR MOM

june

1

I LONG FOR THE ROOF TO CAVE IN AT KEEHN'S department store. For a bomb threat. Or even for a simple power outage. Anything to stop the torture of swimsuit shopping with my mother.

"What about this one?" Mom holds up a tiny orange polka dot bikini.

Skimpy. They are *all* skimpy.

I stare at her. Is she crazy? That is not going to fit me. And even if Keehn's did have my size, it would be a crime against humanity to show that much flab in public. Judging by the look on the practically concave saleswoman's face—the one who scanned me up and down and is now comparing my measurements to the orange Band-Aids with strings my mom is holding—I am not the only one who thinks this.

"What?" asks Mom.

"Nothing." I shake my head and pretend to browse. It's not worth going into it. I don't want to make a scene. Besides, Mom has no clue. How could she? Even when she was eight months pregnant with the twins, she wore size medium maternity clothes. I was twelve then, trying to camouflage my growing curves under large tees. She shrieked about how she had never worn a medium in her life and referred to herself as a cow. Ever since then, I've removed all the size tags from my clothes.

She holds it up to herself. "It's so cute."

"Go for it," I say.

"I would, in a heartbeat." She pinches the skin on her flat belly. "If it weren't for this paunch. And these stretch marks. Nobody wants to see that. Hideous."

Paunch? Yeah, right. Nobody wants to see outright flab, either. I have eyes. I know that I'm bigger than she is. If she believes *she's* hideously fat, what could she possibly think about me? I don't say any of that, though. She'd call me a smart-ass. Maybe I am. But I'm hungry, and tired of pretending to look for something I'm never going to find.

Then she leans in close, still holding the bikini, and puts her arm around me. I'm sure she thinks she's being discreet, but people are watching. She whispers, "With a little effort, you could be in this suit in no time. If you want, I'll get it for you. As incentive."

Incentive? More like a daily reminder of what I'm not.

"No." I pull away and untangle two hangers. "It's okay."

"We could go back to Weight Watchers," she suggests, still whispering.

Been there, done that—four different times since I was ten. I'd lose a little, only to gain it back and then some. Besides, who is she kidding? We both know she's not allowed to join, because she's not overweight. She's not even on the high side of her normal range.

4

We means *I* join and *she* polices every morsel I put in my mouth. No thanks.

"What if I—"

"No!" I cut her off.

A tiny gray-haired woman browsing the rack scowls at me. I look away.

The summer between middle school and high school, Mom wasn't just a realtor but also my personal chef and trainer—or "food and fitness Nazi," as my friend Cassie called her. Her plan to teach me portion control and endorphin euphoria wound up teaching me how to sneak junk food and fake injury. I gained five pounds. After the full physical and thyroid test Mom insisted on came back normal, she gave up.

Or maybe I did.

"Hey, Ann!" My stepsister Naomi and her friend Amber stand by the dressing rooms, each with several tiny, strappy bathing suits. They both give me fakey half-hugs. Typical Naomi: huggy and friendly in public, but if I were at her house, she could go days without saying anything to me—nothing nice, anyway.

Did they see Mom's *incentive* display or hear us discussing Weight Watchers? Oh, God, I hope not. I don't move a muscle. I can feel Mom staring. I pray again for a power outage. Something. Anything to keep her from saying something snide about Dad or his wife Nancy, Naomi's mother.

"How's your summer been?" Amber asks the generic running-into-someone-from-school question. Then she laughs. School's only been out for a couple days.

"Fine, so far." I lean on an overstuffed clearance rack, and several ugly sweaters fall to the floor. "How about you guys?"

"Same." Naomi eyes the full dressing rooms.

"Oh, Naomi!" says Mom. *Oh, God! Kill me now.* "I haven't seen you in years. You've grown into such a *lovely* young woman." Her tone is less than genuine.

"Thanks."

A few months after my parents split up, Dad married his secretary, Nancy, merging the Galardis—Dad, my older brother Tony, and me—with the Thompsons—Nancy, Nate, and Naomi— and built a big, new house across town. Even though Tony and I used to have regular visitation, I haven't spent any real time with Dad in at least a year.

A girl opens a dressing stall door and squeezes past us with her arms full of clothes.

"Come in with me, Amber." Naomi steps into the stall but maintains eye contact with me. "Help me find something that doesn't make my *thighs* look *huge.*"

I pick up a woolly chartreuse sweater from the floor and pretend I didn't hear the thigh comment. I know it's aimed at me. Naomi and her brother Nate called me Thunder Thighs when we were younger. I went home crying more than once because of it. Besides, if Naomi's really *were* big, she'd never want someone in the dressing room with her. Seeing her in her underwear. Or worse, naked.

Amber follows her and laughs. "Like that's possible."

Naomi swats her with a pink bikini top. "Shut up."

"Good luck with that," says Mom, drippy sweet, laced with venom. She must've picked up on Naomi's slam, too. "Tell your mother I said hello."

"Uh-huh."

"Good to see you, Ann," says Amber as Naomi closes the door.

"You too," I say before hurrying back to the swimsuit rack.

"Naomi looks just like her mother." Mom starts in. "Maybe your dad will get *her* a new nose and a set of boobs, too."

"Mom!"

Dad left when I was two. Shouldn't she let it go by now? After all, she and Mike have been married for five years.

"You're right. I'm sorry." Mom looks at the price tag on a floral blouse. "He'd never do that." She wrinkles her nose and drops the tag. "He's too damn cheap."

"Mom! Stop!"

"Okay, okay." She holds a maxi dress in front of her. The bottom drags on the floor. "What's up with Cassie lately?" She puts it back and returns to the bathing suits.

"I don't know." I am not going to talk about Cassie. Especially since I don't really understand what's going on myself.

"Do you like this one?" Mom holds up a putrid green, weirdly cut one-piece. I shake my head. "I just haven't seen her around much. Why don't you invite her to a movie or something?"

I shrug. Even though she lives close by, Cassie and I don't hang out much anymore. Last year, she switched high schools so she could play tennis. We're still Facebook friends, and we still text sometimes, but now she spends most of her time with her teammates, not me.

It's not that big a deal really, but Mom acts like it's a crime to not have an active social life. Doesn't she get it? I can't just walk into Keehn's and pick a new best friend off the rack. I have a hard enough time finding a bathing suit.

In between a frumpy floral one-piece and a mesh cover-up, I

find a tankini that's kind of cute. It has a coral, teal, and brown-striped top and brown shorts—chocolate brown, like my hair, with a matching striped belt. I could see myself wearing that on the beach without a ton of embarrassment. They even have my size. I start to perk up. Finally, a possibility.

"What about this?"

"Antoinette! Come on." She grabs the tag. "You're not a seventeen! That thing is huge! Don't they have a smaller one?"

A smaller one won't cover my ass. Are you blind, Mom?

For the record: I *am* a seventeen.

This is why I cut the tags out of my clothes and prefer to shop alone.

I catch people looking away. Like they feel sorry for us—either because I can't fit into a cute swimsuit or because Mom has to deal with a fat daughter. I'm not sure which, but it doesn't matter. My face is hot. I'm sure it's red. I hate that my face always gives me away. All I want is for the earth to open up and swallow me whole.

Resolving to wear a T-shirt and shorts again this summer and avoid swimming altogether, I slip the suit back on the rack and walk away.

2

AFTER WANDERING AROUND THE MALL FOR A while, I end up at Snapz! The coolest place in the world to shop. The latest styles in the trendiest colors. They even have their own sizing: negative three fits sizes zero or one; negative two is for one to three; negative one is three to five; zero is actually five to seven; their size one is seven to nine; size two is nine to eleven; and size three is eleven to thirteen.

A *sliding scale to boost girls' self-esteem*, Mom said when the store first opened last year and an article explained their "unique sizing." Even so, I'd need about a five. Maybe a four, but probably five. It doesn't matter. They don't have either one, which does nothing for *my* self-esteem.

If I worked at Snapz!, though, I would be instantly cool. And my social life would go from nonexistent to persistent. At school, the girls who wear their clothes stand out, and the lucky few who have jobs there are invited to every party. Everyone seems to want to hang out with them. Probably in case they give gift cards as gifts, but still. Being popular is a curse I wouldn't mind having.

It's not like I'm considered a loser at school or anything. People talk to me—we've all grown up together. It's just I'm not in any group. There are a few others who don't fit in, either, but most of them are shy and prefer to eat alone. Cassie and I used to sit with lots of different people at lunch—usually the artsy theater kids or the band members, but sometimes the cheerleaders or the student council—but now it's just me. I still sit with the same groups but rarely have much to say, because I wasn't with them at practice or at the parties over the weekend. I don't get their inside jokes, so I listen and eat and basically blend in with the orange plastic cafeteria seats.

I spot a bright, multicolored summer dress from the Snapz! website, one I've been drooling over for weeks. I want to try it on. Do I dare? It won't fit. They don't make my size. But it's made with stretchy fabric. Maybe it would. Maybe this time it will.

I reach into the back of the display—the bigger sizes are always toward the back—and pull out a three, and I stroll back to the dressing rooms like trying on clothes here is something I do all the time. A salesgirl opens one of the hot pink louver doors. I smile, thank her, go in, and lock the door behind me.

I slip off my flip-flops and capris and take off my shirt. I slide the little straps off the hanger and hold the dress up to me. Sure, it doesn't cover everything, but it's not on yet. I yank on it a little. It's pretty elastic. I stretch it out even more, just to be sure. First, I try to step into it and pull it up, but the waist won't go over my hips and butt. That's okay. I'll try putting it on over my head. I imagine watching it drape perfectly, like something out of a commercial.

I bunch up the dress and slip one arm through. I put both arms up over my head to push the other one through. The dress slides down and smashes both arms to my ears like a rubber band. I wiggle and wiggle, trying to get some part of it to fall toward my shoulders, so I can free one or both of my arms.

What was I thinking, trying on a dress two sizes too small? *Stupid, stupid, stupid.* Gram always says, *You can't put ten pounds of crap in a five-pound bag.* The same is true with flab.

I sigh and hop and wiggle some more. I know my arms are visible from the outside of the dressing room. Both sticking straight up. I wonder if people can also see some of the fabric that is holding me hostage. Probably.

So I panic. I jump and writhe and grunt and try forcing my arms down. The dress is over my face, so I bump into the dressing room walls. I whack my elbow pretty hard. It hurts. I'm sweating, and my face burns red-hot, again.

All of a sudden, my phone rings. My ringtone for Mom is a loud funky disco song. I struggle and fumble around, but there is no way I can answer it. The song plays three loops before it stops.

A knock at the door startles me. "Are you okay?"

"Um, yeah," I manage.

"Do you need any help?"

"No. Everything's fine. A-okay in here." I pretend nothing is wrong but end up sounding high-pitched and crazy. All the while I'm thrashing and bumping into every side of the stall, which is making me claustrophobic. What I really want to say is, *Call 9-1-1 and have them bring the Jaws of Life to cut me out of here.*

I imagine the call now:

9-1-1. State your emergency.

We have a girl here trapped in a dress.

Excuse me?

Yes, you heard right. A girl trapped in a dress. A fat girl. Trapped in a Snapz! size 3.

Really? Whatever compelled her to do that?

That's what everyone will want to know. The operator. The sales staff. The news crews and anchors. Mom. Me. What *was* I thinking?

Finally, and quite by accident, the dress disguised as a vise gets caught on a hook, which I use to pry it from my head and free my arms. But not without a lot of deep sighing and more grunting. These are not sounds you want to make in public, not ever.

When I'm free, I throw the multicolored wad to the ground and exhale. My face is red and sweaty and my hair is a mess. I take a few deep breaths, then dress and smooth my hair with my hands. I put the mangled dress back on the hanger and emerge from the dressing room—to an audience. People browse racks and pretend they're not watching me, but I know they are. I see the awkward sideways glances and tight lips, probably holding back laughter. I put the dress on the first rack I see and beeline for the door.

Mom is heading toward me from three stores down. "Where have you been?" she asks when she gets closer.

I shrug.

"What do you mean you don't know?" She looks confused, irritated. "I've been looking all over Keehn's for you! I tried calling and you didn't answer. And what's wrong with you? You look out of breath and sweaty. Are you okay? Are you sick?"

"I'm fine," I mutter and walk away, fighting back tears.

"Did you find anything?" Mom catches up.

"No," I say. "Nothing."

"Did you look in that Snapz! store? They have some cute things."

I can't answer her. If I do, I won't be able to hold it together. I know it. I do not want to cry at the mall. I do not. I breathe in slowly and exhale. Walk and breathe. Walk and breathe. I push away all thoughts of bathing suits and dresses and judgmental looks. All thoughts of being trapped in dressing rooms and dresses and flabby bodies. All thoughts of frustration and embarrassment and self-loathing.

Instead I think about lunch. Chicken parmesan and breadsticks.

3

WE MEET MIKE AND THE TWINS IN THE FOOD
court for lunch. The moment I've been waiting for. Mini versions
of my favorite restaurants all lined up. The light at the end of the
shopping tunnel. I'm starving. They are already at a table, the
twins picking at their chicken strips and fries, and Mike with a
cheeseburger, onion rings, and his phone—downloading newspa-
pers for later, no doubt. Next to his tray is a salad, still covered.

"Ann! Ann!" Libby wiggles her fingers in my face. One finger
has an oversize red plastic ring on it. "See what Daddy bought me?"

"Yup." Like I care.

Mike stands and kisses Mom. "Did you girls have fun?"

"Uh-huh," I say. "Loads."

Mike looks at Mom. She gives him an I'll-tell-you-later look.

Judd pulls a blue marbled rubber ball from his pocket. "Look. I
got this. It goes real high."

"Great," I say sarcastically.

"Be nice," warns Mom.

"I got you that salad with the strawberries," Mike tells Mom.

"And before you say anything—yes, the fat-free raspberry vinaigrette is on the side."

"Ooh, my hero!" She sits down and pops the plastic lid off the salad.

Mike hands me a twenty-dollar bill. "I didn't know what you wanted. You're not as predictable as your mother." He smiles.

"Thanks." I walk toward the Napanelli's booth, glad that Mike didn't just order me a cheeseburger, like he sometimes does.

Before I get out of earshot, Mike asks Mom, "So? Did you buy anything?"

From the line, I can see Mom is talking a mile a minute. I don't need to hear what she's saying. I know. She's telling him how she offered to buy me any suit I wanted, even one that didn't fit, as incentive. How I was impossible to please. How I walked away and sulked. How I disappeared and didn't answer my cell when she called. How I don't appreciate all she tries to do.

I *do* appreciate it. I just wish she wouldn't try so hard.

A group of kids from school is at another table in the food court. They wave. I wave and smile back. If I were with Cassie, we'd go over and sit down, without question. Cassie is outgoing—always putting herself at the center of attention, whether people want her there or not.

Eagle-eye Mom notices and motions for me to go over there. I wish she'd stop pushing. I will not be a desperate wannabe who gloms onto people and ingratiates herself into conversations. I'd rather eat lunch with my family at the mall than tag along with people who didn't invite me.

I pretend I don't see Mom. The line inches forward. A girl—a redhead, about ten or so—and some guy—probably her dad—are ahead of me. I was her age the first time I met Mike, right here in the food court.

I'd just taken a bite of my pepperoni pizza and burned my tongue when he walked up and hugged Mom. Tony wanted to punch him from the get-go, but I was too busy fishing ice out of my pop to soothe my tongue to realize right away what was going on. She'd sold him the house we live in now, and he asked her out. They'd dated for weeks before Tony and I met him. Mike was all smiles and bought us ice cream after lunch. A year later, they were married, and we no longer had Mom to ourselves.

I look at the menu and try to decide. Not what I want to eat. I already know that—a large chicken parm with extra breadsticks. I'm trying to decide whether it's worth Mom's do-you-really-want-all-that look.

Maybe I should order a salad. According to *Slimmer You*, the dieting handbook that I have read cover-to-cover umpteen times since I was ten, "When dining out, you should always order with your head and not your stomach. Do not allow hunger to bully common sense."

The line moves. The girl orders pepperoni pizza. I want to tell her to let it cool before she takes a bite, but I don't.

At the table Mike is wiping his pants with a napkin, and Mom and the twins are laughing. The Logan family: Michael, the local lawyer gearing up for his second run at the Michigan House of Representatives; his lovely wife, Suzanne, winner of last year's Jackson County Realtor of the Year; and their adorable, tow-headed four-year-old twins, Justice and Liberty. Somehow mousy-haired Antoinette Galardi doesn't quite fit in that perfect image. Especially now that Tony's out of the picture.

Then I see something I hadn't noticed before. There are only four chairs at the table.

"Can I help you?" The person behind the counter is talking to me.

"Um, yeah." I look back at the table.

The Logans. Four chairs. All filled.

"Yeah. I'll take a large chicken parmesan with extra bread-sticks." Hunger shoves common sense into the dirt.

"Anything else?"

"Yeah. A slice of strawberry cheesecake." And kicks her while she's down.

"Is that for here or to go?" she asks.

I look back. Mike is throwing away the kids' barely touched chicken, and Mom is pushing away her salad. I can almost hear her saying that she couldn't eat another bite. Of course they'll wait for me, and squeeze in another chair, but I don't want them to. I need to get out of there. Away from the mall and away from them.

"To go," I say. "Thanks."

4

AFTER WE LEAVE THE MALL, I ASK MOM AND MIKE to drop me at Gram's. "I'll walk home later," I tell them.

"Leave your attitude there," Mom tells me as the minivan door closes.

I guess I'll be there a while.

I key the security code into the pad. The garage opens. I knock twice and walk in, so Gram knows it's me and doesn't freak.

"Hey, Ann," she says from the laundry room. "I'll be there in a minute. Just finishing up a load."

"Okay." I plop in front of the TV, turn it on, and open the take-out bag. Tangy sauce and garlic scents mix with the smell of Gram's house—cigarette smoke covered by Lemon Pledge, Opium perfume, and sweet vanilla room freshener—and all is right with the world.

Gram's is home. Not the address on my driver's license kind of home, but the place Tony and I logged in more childhood hours, both good and bad, than anywhere else. After Dad and before Mike—that is, from ages two to ten for me, ages five to thirteen for Tony, Mom worked weird hours. Sometimes she did office work for a temp agency; sometimes she waited tables; sometimes both. Dad was preoccupied with his new family and climbing the corporate ladder at Arrowhead Steel. So we were dumped at Gram's.

I remember running around and around the kitchen island with Tony, until we collapsed. Making candies and butterscotch pie with Gram. Sleeping in our "fort," the dining room table with a blanket draped over it. Watching classic horror movies and making fun of reality TV with Uncle Doug. Reading, curled up in the recliner in the corner—*Gramps's chair*, Gram calls it—while Tony mastered Super Mario Bros.

We lived here for most of the summer before I started fourth grade. No one told us where Mom was. I cried night after night, thinking she was never coming back. Tony would climb in my bed and tell funny stories he'd made up until I started laughing and Gram yelled at us. I'd beg him to stay with me, and he said he would. Pinky swore. But when I woke up, he was always back in his own bed. Tony left, even though he promised.

Mom did come back. But she focused on her real estate career, and Gram picked up the slack—again.

That was then. Chicken parm is now.

After grabbing a pop from the fridge, I cut the chicken into uniform pieces. Creating perfect bites—a chunk of chicken with saucy pasta twirled around it—I channel-surf and stop on an infomercial.

Natalie S. from Battle Creek, Michigan, lost forty-five pounds in twelve weeks. Twelve weeks. Interesting. Natalie S., if that is her real name, lives about an hour from here. She is sixteen and five foot four, just like me. Wow. Her *after* pic is amazing. Could I ever look like that?

I follow a perfect bite with another and another, and then part of a breadstick and some pop.

I get so engrossed in Natalie S.'s story and perfect bites that I barely notice Gram sit down and light a cigarette. She holds it near the open window and exhales in that direction, too, but I still smell it. I hate that she smokes, but I don't say anything because she's tried quitting more times than I've tried dieting. I may not know the secret to self-control, but I do know that guilt trips do not work.

"Where's your car?" Gram blows smoke out the window. She gave Tony and me her old Corolla when she upgraded a couple of years ago. Tony bought a newer car after graduation, so now it's mine.

"Mom and Mike dropped me off." I don't take my eyes off the TV. "Nice day for a walk." She doesn't press me to tell her more, so I don't.

I've seen a thousand fitness and weight loss infomercials, but this one hits home. Maybe it's because Natalie S. is so much like me. Maybe I'm tired of feeling like crap and ready to do something about it for real this time. Maybe I'm grasping at straws. Who knows, but still I can't help fantasizing about this program. About it working. If so, in three measly months—by the end of summer—I could look like Natalie S's *after* picture. Thin. Confident. Happy.

I shove the empty entrée container into the paper bag and wad it tight. I'm stuffed, which is when I usually think about starting a new diet.

The first thing I have to do is order the S2S (Secrets 2 Success) Weight Loss System for five payments of $19.99. The first step to the rest of my life.

"Hey, Gram, can I borrow your credit card? I don't have my debit card with me."

"What for?"

I start to answer her, but then I see what she's wearing. The bright floral scoop-neck blouse and navy blue gauchos, the long strand of hot pink beads, matching pink lipstick, and several large, gaudy rings are typical, but the yellow and white striped knee socks—yes! knee socks!—white beret, and braids catch me off guard.

"Don't *you* look like the cat's pajamas today," I say, which is what she always tells me when I'm dressed up—or sometimes sarcastically, if I'm dressed down.

"Cat pajamas—great! Just the look I was going for." Which is what I always say back to her. "What did you want my credit card for?" She's cross-legged on the couch with her cigarette paused at her puckered lips, as if she can't take a drag until I answer her question.

The TV prompts me. "This revolutionary new weight loss system." I say. "I'll pay you back."

"Oh, yeah?" She inhales, brightening the tip of her cigarette.

"Yeah. Only five payments of nineteen ninety-nine." I mimic the TV announcer. "Wait. They'll make the first payment for me. That's only four payments. Better yet."

"And what does that eighty bucks buy?" She sounds skeptical. I understand. She hasn't seen the whole infomercial. If she had seen the *before* and *after* pics of Natalie S. and the tears as she told her story, she'd be on board.

"A customized diet guide for my unique metabolism, a workout DVD with resistance bands, two whole weeks' worth of food—frozen and pre-packaged—and a 30-day supply of supplements—"

"Pills?" Gram cuts in. "Do you have idea how dangerous some of that garbage is?"

"They're nutritional supplements," I say in my normal voice. "All natural."

She flicks ashes into the ashtray. "These things are natural, too." She laughs and then coughs. A deep, craggy cough. "Natural"—*cough*—"doesn't"—*cough*—"always"—*cough*—"mean"—*cough*—"good for you."

Holy shit. Has Gram always coughed like that?

"You okay?" I say.

"Aw, hell, I'm fine." She is flushed. "Just a little tickle."

"Maybe you should see a doctor."

"What for? He'll just tell me to quit smoking."

I look at her, not wanting to nag, but even she has to realize how ridiculous that is.

"Think about it," she says. "A two-hundred-and-some-pound fat ass waddles into the doctor's office complaining that her knees ache. What's he gonna do? Tell her to lose weight. Right? But she thinks she can't because she can't exercise because her knees ache. She leaves crying and ends up polishing off two pints of Häagen-Däzs. Is she better off?"

Gram calls pretty much everyone *fat ass*, especially those she doesn't know or like. (Never me or anyone else she loves.) Mom once asked her to stop, saying it would give me a complex. I'm not sure what's worse: Gram calling everyone fat asses or Mom confirming that I have a fat ass by asking Gram not to call attention to it.

"Maybe the doctor can give her a new diet pill that just came out, or suggest one of those surgeries, or a low-impact exercise program. I dunno," I say. "And maybe he could give *you* an inhaler or something."

She smiles.

I grin back. *I've got you there, Gram, and you know it.*

"I've got my inhaler right here." She takes a deep drag on her cigarette. "Those doctors don't know squat. Just a week before my Joe dropped dead from a heart attack—God rest his soul—the doctor gave him a clean bill of health. Clean bill of health, my ass! That man ate bacon every day of his life. Didn't take a genius to know his arteries were practically solid. But he lived life to the fullest, on his own terms, and by God, I do, too."

There is no reasoning with Gram when she starts in. Gramps died a year before I was born, and I've heard the bacon-and-clean-bill-of-health story no less than two hundred times. Mom cringes whenever she starts in, because it sounds like Gram doesn't care that he's gone. But Aunt Jackie says it's her way of coping. That nobody could ever love anyone as much as Gram and Gramps loved each other. They look so happy in the picture on the TV cabinet. Every time I look at it, I wish that I'd known him and seen the two of them together—an example of lifelong love. Besides, bacon every day sounds pretty good.

"Act now," the TV announcer says. "This is a limited time offer."

"So can I borrow your credit card?" I say. "I have the money in my bank account to pay you back."

Gram sighs, sets her cigarette in her ashtray, and yanks up a knee sock. "You already know more than those people. You don't need that. Besides, you're perfect just as you are."

"Psssht," I say. "Not according to the ideal weight chart. I need to lose forty-five pounds, at least."

"Ha! Those things don't take real people into account. They just make you fork out more money for gimmicks, like those things you've already tried."

I dig my toe into the thick burgundy carpet and remember the juice diet, the zero-carb diet, and the shake diet. "Just because I couldn't stick to them doesn't mean they're gimmicks."

Gram scoots to the edge of the couch and leans forward to squeeze my hand. "That's exactly why they're gimmicks. *Nobody* could stick to them. They're poppycock!"

I burst out laughing. "Poppycock?"

"Don't be hatin' on my BBC vocabulary." Gram strikes a pose. Is she supposed to be a British aristocrat or a gangsta?

"Gram, you need to stop watching so much TV. You're mixing up your slang."

"I'm not the one who needs to stop watching TV, missy." She nods toward the infomercial.

"But what if this is the diet that will finally work for me? *Slimmer You* says to never give up trying."

"See what I mean?" She puts her cigarette out—another crumpled, lipstick-stained corpse in the ashtray graveyard—grabs the remote, and turns off the TV. "You already have every diet book and chart memorized. When you put your mind to losing weight—truly put your mind to it—you won't need gimmicky programs and pills. You'll do it when you're ready. With what you already know."

"Think so?"

"Know so," she says.

"How can you be so sure?"

"Because you're just like me." Gram lights another cigarette and changes the subject. "So, how was shopping?"

I tell her everything. About the bikini and the incentive and the huge striped suit. About seeing Naomi and what Mom said. She listens but doesn't take sides.

She does speak her mind about the bathing suit, though. "Why don't you buy that suit yourself? Who cares if your mom likes it? *She's* not the one wearing it."

I wish I didn't care. But I couldn't put that suit on without hearing my mother's disgust that I'm a size seventeen. I'd rather spend my money losing weight so I can buy a smaller, worthy-of-keeping-the-size-tag-intact suit.

The talk turns to Cassie. All Gram says is, "Friends come into your life, and then they go. You're just in a transition. Nothing to worry about."

If only Mom could hear that.

My story stops at the food court, so I don't tell her *everything*. When I'm done, I eat the cheesecake. I don't know why. I'm still stuffed, and it doesn't even taste that great. As I shovel forkful after forkful into my mouth, I think about Natalie S. I can't help but wonder if I've missed out on the first step to the rest of my life.

5

A COUPLE OF NIGHTS LATER I SIT AT THE DINNER table, considering my mashed potato options. Do I really want more? According to *Slimmer You*, I should "wait a full twenty minutes before taking seconds. Sip water while you wait. During that time your brain will register that you're full." Is another helping worth Mom's disapproving look or, worse, her saying, *Do you* really need *all of that?* Or would she even notice?

"What's going on this weekend, Suz?" Mike asks her.

"I don't know. Why?"

I take a swig of water and wait, eyeing Mom's plate. The dab of potatoes is so minuscule that it barely counts. It's untouched. I hate how in control she is. A perfect size six, never a hair out of place or a chipped nail. Even the house is perfect. I defy anyone to find a dust bunny or cobweb around here—except for my room, which is a disaster area. She is so manic and anal. I can't take it sometimes.

That's probably why Dad left her. I don't remember the details, of course, because I was two. But I do remember when Tony left, since it was just a year ago.

Tony was thirteen when Mom married Mike. Aunt Jackie said he was threatened by Mike since he had always been the "man of the house." Gram said he just loved pushing people's buttons. Mom called him an instigator. Whatever it was, he did the opposite of everything Mike told him to do. By the time the twins came along, Mike was fed up. There was constant fighting. Tony and Mike. Mike and Mom. Mom and Tony. I tried to stay out of it, but the endless tension had me pretty keyed up. Mondo Burgers, Little Debbie's snack cakes, and Cheetos were my Xanax.

Eventually Tony went to live at Dad and Nancy's, while I continued the usual visitation Wednesday night and every other weekend. Everything was fine for a while. Then Nancy had a baby—Noah—and started going to church all the time. She transformed from a selfish lizard to a Bible-breathing monster, so Tony started calling her Godzilla behind her back. She wigged out about everything from rock music and R-rated movies to piercings and swearing.

Tony, being the button-pushing instigator, harassed Nancy even more than he did Mike. Partly because she was so easy to freak out but mainly because Dad started blowing us off. Wednesday night church services and weekend business travel and sporting events for Nate and Naomi reduced my visits to a couple of times a month, tops. Tony took it out on Nancy, not Dad.

The big blow-up came about a year ago, right after Tony's high school graduation. He called Nancy a hypocrite, saying it was one thing for her to believe in God, but for her to be so rigid and judgmental when she'd started screwing around with Dad—*didn't the Bible call that adultery?* he asked—while they were both still married was f-ing wrong (except he said the whole word). The kicker was that he said it all in front of Nate and Naomi. Godzilla lost it. She booted Tony out, and Dad never said a word.

Mom heard that Tony was staying with friends until he moved into the dorms at Grand Valley State, but he refused to see her or answer her calls or emails. Mike said that he'd contact us when it was time to pay tuition, but he was wrong. Even though it's only a few hours away, Tony hasn't been back. He still won't talk to any of us.

Not even me.

I haven't been over to Dad's since, and he's never even called to ask why. It pisses me off how easily Mom and Dad have both moved on from the family they screwed up to start fresh ones.

I take another sip of water. It doesn't help. I still want more potatoes. I think about the Secrets 2 Success Weight Loss System again, about Natalie S., and whether it's the right program at the right time. The one that will work. Should I mention it to Mom? I hate talking with her about diets, but she does know a lot about them. Maybe just ask if she's heard of it. The mashed potatoes taunt me with their fluffiness. It's now or never.

"Mom . . ." I say.

"Mommy, look," says Libby. "My smashed tatoes look like a crown."

"Mine look like a cloud," says Judd.

Our toy poodle, Gigi, poises herself between the twins, ready for scraps to fall.

"Well, my mother called today." Mike shovels a forkful into his mouth. Waiting for a reaction from Mom, I'm guessing.

Mom exhales loudly. "Okay . . . what did she—Liberty! Don't fling your peas on the floor."

"But I hate them," says Libby.

"She's coming to town this weekend," Mike says, his mouth full. He mumbles something else that I can't understand. Shouldn't the future Representative of the 65th District know how to eat and talk at the same time?

"I don't want my peas, either," says Judd.

"And she wants to stay with us overnight," Mike continues, after he swallows. Now *that* I understood. Mom's attention is about to be derailed. I need to hurry.

"Mom . . ." I try again.

"Hmm?" Mom answers. Is she talking to me or someone else?

"When I was at Gram's today," I say, "there was this infomercial . . ."

"Do I have to eat them?" asks Libby.

"I'm full," says Judd.

Mom reaches over and places several peas on top of Libby's mashed potatoes. "See? They're jewels on your crown. Eat the yummy jewels, Lib."

Hello? Who cares whether or not Libby eats her peas? I'm trying to talk to you, Mom.

"I don't wanna," says Libby. "They're yucky."

"What about mine?" asks Judd. "Are my peas jewels, too?"

"Your peas are little poops," says Libby.

"Mom!" Judd screams. "Libby called my peas poops!"

I reach across the table, plop a big spoonful of potatoes on my plate, and take a bite. It hasn't been twenty minutes, but I don't care. If I were Tony, I'd stand up and make a scene. But I'm not Tony.

Mom glances at me but says nothing. She walks over to the sink, wets a paper towel, and wipes the twins' mouths and hands. "Liberty, Justice, you're done. Go play." The twins jump down and run to the family room, and Gigi follows. Mom scrapes their plates and puts them in the sink.

I shovel more potatoes into my mouth. Soft, buttery warmth.

"Well, what should I tell her?" says Mike. "She wants me to call her back tonight."

"What?" asks Mom. "Who?"

"My mother," says Mike. "Coming to stay with us on her way to Aunt Carol's this weekend."

"*This* weekend?" screeches Mom. "I don't have time to clean—"

Mike cuts her off. "I'll help. The house looks great, Suz. You do such a great job." *Suck-up.* "She'll only be here overnight. She won't notice if the house isn't perfect."

Mom gives Mike her are-you-crazy? look. She'll notice. Mom knows it. I know it. And Mike knows it, too. When I said I defy anyone to find a dust bunny or a cobweb in this house, I didn't include Regina Logan. She is not just *anyone*. She's Queen Critical. If you look up critical in the dictionary, there's a picture of her— *One that a monkey could take better*, she'd say.

Maybe I'll spend the weekend with Gram.

6

THE NEXT AFTERNOON I GIVE GRAM A CALL.

"He-llooo," she croons.

"Hey, Gram. What's up?"

"Just a few Japanese beetles sizzling in the light fixture," she says. She always does that. She actually looks up and reports what she sees.

"Nice," I say. "What are you doing this weekend?"

Before she answers, I hear her take a drag of a cigarette. "Headed to the casino in Sault Ste. Marie with Maureen and her fat-ass sister. Going to win big. I feel it in my bones."

Maureen has been Gram's best friend ever since Mom was a baby. They both smoke like chimneys, swear like truck drivers, and gamble every chance they get. Gram has never liked Maureen's sister, saying she's a tagalong leech, and, of course, a fat ass.

"You sure that feeling's not just arthritis?" I ask.

"Aw, hell," she says, laughing. Then she has a coughing fit so loud I have to take the phone away from my ear.

"Do you need someone to stay at your house and keep an eye on things, feed your fish, water your flowers, and stuff?"

"Got someone." She inhales again. "Doug says he's fumigating his apartment. More like avoiding his fat-ass girlfriend, if you want my opinion. But that's none of my business."

Damn! Uncle Doug beat me to it. He probably *is* fighting with Tayla. They fight all the time. But he's a lot more fun than Regina.

He lived with Gram up until a few years ago. When I was younger and we stayed over, I'd sit up late and watch DVDs with him—mostly horror movies from the eighties and nineties, but a lot of Alfred Hitchcock, too. Mom would get so mad, saying they'd give me nightmares. But Uncle Doug made fun of the music, the cheesy special effects, and the overacting. Until I was twelve, I thought they were comedies.

"I'll probably have to have *my* place fumigated when I get back," says Gram, "after two days of Doug stinking it up with chili dogs and cheap beer farts."

TMI, Gram. Too much information. A horror movie marathon just lost all its appeal. And I can't stay with Aunt Jackie and Chris because they have a cat. The last time I spent the night there, my eyes swelled shut and I wheezed for days.

"Thanks for asking though, kiddo."

"Yeah," I say. "No problem. Have fun at the casino. Bring me back some fudge."

"Will do." Gram hangs up. No good-bye. Just a cough and a *clunk*. I'm used to it.

I pick up the remote and flip through the stations. Nothing good is ever on TV in the afternoons, but I go through the motions anyway. I settle on a movie I've seen no less than a thousand times.

It's more than halfway through, but I don't care. I already know what happens.

"Ann," Mom calls from the kitchen, "we're going for a family bike ride. Want to come?"

I turn down the TV and take my feet off the coffee table in case she comes in. "No," I say, and quickly add, "thanks, anyway." It's supposed to be almost ninety outside today. Air-conditioning is my friend; sweating is not.

"Come on." She pops her head around the doorway. "It's a beautiful day. It'll do you good to get off the couch and get some fresh air." She's decked out in black bike shorts and a fitted white tank top, her trusty crusty running shoes, and a terry cloth headband. Fashion Plate Barbie rides her bike.

I stopped riding a bike in fourth grade. That was when I grew pup tent boobs and got muffin top love handles instead of hips. *Early bloomer*, Gram said. *Puberty*, Mom said. I hated that word. Still do. Bra shopping with Mom was worse than swimsuit shopping. It's a wonder I don't break out in a cold sweat at the mere mention of the mall.

Within hours of my wearing my first bra to school, Vinnie Romero, who sat directly behind me, discovered it; he saw the outline through my shirt. Every few hours he'd reach out, yank on the back, and let go. *Snap!* Not only did it hurt, but everyone laughed. Everyone but Cassie. She told the teacher. Vinnie got in trouble, but it didn't stop him.

That same week, I noticed that when I kicked a ball, ran, jumped, or even rode my bike over rough pavement or gravel, all my new protrusions jiggled. I felt like a walking tub of Jell-O. Topped with Cool Whip. So I stopped doing all those things and came up with any excuse possible to get out of public displays of jiggling: headache, stomachache, fake ankle injury, and when all else failed—cramps.

Mom bought it for a while and wrote notes—aka excused absences—to get me out of gym class. Eventually she caught on and would tell me that *this* note was the last one, but it never was. I would cry and refuse to go to school, and she would cave. Just like she does now with the twins and junk food.

Tony stuck up for me whenever Naomi said that if I'd get off my lazy butt more, maybe I wouldn't have thunder thighs. Nate would laugh, and Tony would punch him. Then I'd call Mom crying, and she'd come get us—usually with a few choice words for Dad and Nancy.

The ironic thing is that the longer I avoided the jiggle, the more jiggle there was. So now I'm not only self-conscious about that, but also about what people might think if I got on a bike or exercised in public: *Look at that fat ass. . . . I bet she'll pop the tires any second now. . . . It'll take a lot more miles to ride off those Twinkies, sweetheart.* That's how it is. I know this. I've heard Grandma, Maureen, and Aunt Jackie. Even Mom sometimes, although she'd deny it. They don't say it about me. (At least I don't think so.) But they say it about strangers in public. Kind of makes me wonder what people think when they see me. I'm sure it's bad. There are a lot of people out there ruder than my family.

"Are you coming or not?" asks Mom.

"No," I say. "I'm really into this movie."

"Suit yourself," she says. The door slams.

I don't know what's worse: my imagining what others think of me on a bike or what I know my mother thinks about me sitting on the couch in front of the TV on a nice day.

I change the channel to another movie. An old one, but new to me. And, ironically, a thin, gorgeous blonde—Meg Ryan, maybe—rides her bike on a country road. She smiles like she has no cares in the world. Like no one ever judges her. Like her life is perfect. Wind through her hair and sunshine on her face. The only thing missing are the rainbows and butterflies and cartoon birds singing on her shoulder.

Maybe I should grab my bike and try to catch up with Mom, Mike, and the kids. They can't be going very fast. I would love to feel like that, even if it's just for a second—free and peaceful and normal.

Suddenly, there's a truck. It can't be headed toward Meg Ryan. Could it? Yes. Oh my God. No! Meg Ryan just got hit by that truck.

Figures. See what happens when you exercise?

MOM HUSTLES ALL WEEK TO MAKE THE HOUSE
perfect. I don't see much difference, because it's pretty much constantly staged and ready to show, even though it's not for sale.
Ultra-modern leather furniture, glass tables, a couple of lamps,
and a few perfectly placed family pictures. That's all. No clutter.
No signs that real people actually live here. *A place for everything,
everything in its place.* Always.

My room is a different story. I only make my bed when I change
my sheets, and I have clothes and shoes everywhere. I'm not a total
slob, though, even if Mom would disagree. No matter how bad it
looks, it really is organized.

I have three different wardrobes for each season.

1. The clothes I actually wear, which are all over my
   floor, bed, and in laundry baskets, because there's
   no room anywhere else.
2. The clothes that will fit if I lose weight. These
   fill the closet and dresser. I don't want to get rid

of them because I hope I'll be back into them someday.

3. The "incentive clothes" Mom has bought me over the years. They hang in the back of the closet, with tags still on them. Some are out of style now, but I don't go looking for them because it's too depressing to think about all the time I've spent being fat.

I have enough shoes, on the other hand, to match all three wardrobes. After all, no matter my pants size, my shoes are always size 7. And they are everywhere. Even though I usually do, Mom stresses repeatedly that I should keep my bedroom door shut while Regina is here.

She sprays Windex, Pledge, 409, and Febreze over everything and wipes and scrubs every hard surface and some soft ones, too. I take Libby to pick up Gigi from the groomer's. She's fluffed and puffed and topped with a pink bow. We vacuum and mop again just before Regina gets here. Even the twins glide dust cloths across everywhere they can reach. Mom is wigging out all over the place, screaming that the whole house is still a mess.

As soon as the doorbell rings on Saturday afternoon, she instantly transforms from Dr. Jekyll to Ms. Hyde. Her voice goes from a loud screech to soft and calm. Her face smooths out. And she actually smiles for the first time all week. Yes, it looks more like a terrified grimace, but I think it's a smile. She reminds me of a director clapping her hands and calling, *Places, everyone.*

Mike answers the door. "Hello, Mother." He kisses her cheek. "Nice to see you." So formal. I shake my head, because if Mom ever kissed Gram or said *Nice to see you* like that, Gram would call her a smart-ass. Better than fat ass, but still not a compliment.

Regina comes in carrying a ham. Yes, a ham. Still wrapped from the grocery store. Gigi dances on her back legs, greeting Regina and sniffing. So what if Gigi's paws touch Regina's knee? She is a dog, after all. That's what dogs do. They sniff things, like guests and hams. She is not being obnoxious at all. But Regina thrusts her leg forward, knocking Gigi back. "No!" she yells. "Get back! Bad dog!" I scoop up Gigi and tuck her under my arm. She tips her head toward my face and licks the air. I take that to mean she's grateful.

The twins stand behind Mom and me, like they've been kicked off Regina's leg themselves. I haven't seen them this quiet since the last time she visited. It kind of freaks me out.

"Oh, a ham." Mom takes it with both hands. "I just made roast beef."

"Yes, I know," says Regina. "Mike told me. But ham is so versatile. We could have sandwiches later and still have enough for a nice breakfast casserole tomorrow morning before I head out to Carol's. It's a long drive to Chicago, so I'll need something substantial to hold me over until mid-afternoon."

Mom hands me the ham, with a nod toward the fridge.

"It's freezing in here." Regina wraps her arms around herself. "Mike, dear, could you grab my bag from the car? I have a sweater in there. Seems I'm going to need it."

"Of course." Mike nearly sprints out of the house.

"Must be nice to be able to have money to throw away on air conditioning." I'm not sure who Regina's talking to, because she doesn't seem to be looking at anyone.

Mom answers anyway. "It was stuffy in here while the roast was in the oven, so I turned up the air." She fiddles with the thermostat in the entryway. "I'll turn it back down."

"Don't do it on my account. I have my sweater. And knit scarf, if need be."

Mom plasters on her fake smile. I try to sneak upstairs to my room, but Mom grabs my arm and tugs me toward the kitchen. Like she needs reinforcements or something.

While Mom and I sweat in the kitchen, Regina pulls her sweater up around her ears. "You know, Suzy, this house would be so much homier with a few knick-knacks around." She readjusts herself on the leather sectional in the family room. "Or maybe a few decorative pillows on this sofa. It's so uncomfortable. They would add a splash of color, too."

Regina's house is practically covered with collectibles—from plates on the wall to porcelain angels on the coffee tables. Worried I might knock something over, I barely breath while I'm there. While she does have pillows in her living room, she comes unglued if anyone moves one. It's pretty, but there's nothing homey about it.

"I'll keep that in mind, Regina." Mom pulls the baked potatoes out of the oven while I slice the meat. Libby and Judd set the table. Mike waits on his mother. She asks him for ginger ale. He says we don't have any, but he could run to the store, if she wants. She says for him not to go to the bother, but he goes anyway. Any excuse to get out of there.

"Do you need any help?" Regina asks. Since the family room, dining area, and kitchen are basically one huge open space, I can tell she has no intention of moving.

"We're fine," says Mom. "Don't worry. Just relax and read your magazine."

Regina always brings women's magazines with her. She flips through the pages and looks up and huffs every time one of the twins scampers and giggles. Or when Mom drops the corn pan into the sink by accident.

Dinner is ready about the time Mike returns with the ginger ale. He pours his mother a glass and puts it at her place at the table.

"What a lovely table," she says as she switches her fork to the left side of her plate and pushes the ginger ale away.

"I did it," says Libby.

"Me, too," says Judd.

Regina doesn't acknowledge them. At least she doesn't tell them that they did it wrong.

"You don't want the ginger ale?" asks Mike.

"Oh, heavens, no. Not with dinner."

Mike looks like a kicked puppy. Like Gigi. I almost feel bad for him. Mom's face is stiff and stony. She glares at Regina and shakes her head with tiny, deliberate movements.

Tension.

When Tony was home, most every dinner was like this. He'd say something to piss off someone. Then he'd sit back and watch the dominoes fall. If I tried to smooth things over, to make everyone stop yelling or staring or slamming, the wrath usually turned on me. While I miss Tony, I do not miss the tension.

"I'd love some ginger ale." I force a fake everything-is-going-to-be-okay-please-don't-yell smile. "Can *I* drink it?"

"May I, dear, not can I," Regina corrects me as she hands the glass across the table. "Be aware that pop packs a wallop with those empty calories."

I force a smile and say, "Yes, I know." I've swallowed a lot in the name of familial peace.

Mike piles roast beef on a plate and passes it to Mom. As the dishes go around the table, Regina says, "Oh my gosh! So much food! Why such a feast, Suzy?"

"We're happy you're here with us, Regina."

"That's nice, dear." Regina takes a tiny bit of everything. "Next time don't go to all the trouble. A ham sandwich and a pickle would do quite nicely." Then she rambles on and on about people from Rochester Hills, where Mike is from. People the rest of us don't know. People Mike doesn't seem to be interested in, but he listens and smiles.

"Please pass the potatoes," I say.

Mike hands them to me. I fork one onto my plate. Officer Mom of the Food Police says nothing. She doesn't need to. Her lieutenant is in town. "Really, Ann," says Regina. "How can you possibly eat that much?"

Mom stares at me like it's my fault for giving Regina reason to criticize. I'm not sure what to say. *It's easy. See?* and gobbling it down doesn't seem polite. But neither is Regina. I look at my plate and contemplate what to do. Ignore her? Put something back? Leave the table? A knock at the back door saves me from having to do or say anything.

Aunt Jackie and her girlfriend, Chris, come in. "Hey," Aunt Jackie says. "Sorry to interrupt dinner."

"No problem," says Mom, clearly relieved. "Grab a seat. We have plenty."

"Hi, Mrs. Logan," Aunt Jackie says to Regina, while Chris smiles and waves. "Nice to see you."

Regina nods, lips pursed. Is that supposed to be a smile?

One part of me wants to hug them both for stopping by. Another part of me wants to yell, *Run! Get out of here! Save yourselves!* Instead I assemble the perfect bite of potato and roast beef on my fork.

Before Aunt Jackie can haul the piano bench to the table, Libby says, "I'm done, Mommy. Can I go play?"

Regina acts like she wants to say something, but she doesn't. There is too much going on with all the clanking of plates and moving around for her to be heard, anyway. She looks like she just sucked on a lemon. I think it's hilarious, but Mike seems panicked.

"Me too," says Judd.

Usually Mom plays the one-more-bite game until they've eaten most of their food, but not today. Instead, while Aunt Jackie and Chris sit down, she takes the twins' plates to the sink and brings back two clean ones. Mom's obviously trying not to smile.

Aunt Jackie and Mom both have long, blonde hair and blue eyes, but that's where the resemblance ends. Jackie's ten years younger, and is calm where my mother is out of control. Her hair is usually pulled up messily in a clip, and her makeup is more natural. She looks just as put-together as Mom, though, if you ask me.

I've liked Chris from the moment I met her. Mom was in labor with the twins, and I was in the family waiting room with Uncle Doug and Tony. Aunt Jackie rushed in with this shorter woman with spiky brown hair. She introduced us before joining Mom, Mike, and Gram.

Chris and I talked, ate Doritos and candy bars from the vending machine, and laughed at Uncle Doug talking to the TV. I loved how she talked to me like a grown-up, not a little kid. How she was a librarian, so she'd not only read my favorite books but told me about others. And how she was a little on the pudgy side, like me.

"So, what's going on?" asks Mom before taking a sip of water.

"Well," says Aunt Jackie, smiling and squeezing Chris's hand. "We just stopped by to tell you that we're getting married."

Mom practically drowns. She coughs and coughs and then laughs. *"What?* Are you serious? When?"

"Oh, wow!" I say. "That is so cool!"

"Congratulations," says Mike.

Regina opens her mouth to speak but closes it again.

"Third weekend in August," Jackie says.

"August?" says Mom. *"This* year?" Jackie nods. "That's only a couple months away. Not much time to plan."

"It's okay. It's going to be small. Simple."

Mom seems skeptical. "I don't know, Jack. There's a lot to do, even if it is small. . . ." I can see her mental checklist forming already.

"Of course, I want you to be my matron of honor." Then Jackie turns to me, "And, Ann, you'll be my bridesmaid, right?"

Me? Really? I'm so stunned—and thrilled—that all I can do is nod.

I've never been a bridesmaid before. Mom and Mike got married in Gram's backyard when I was eleven. It was small and simple, just immediate family and a few friends. We didn't even wear real wedding clothes.

Everyone seems to be talking at once. Mom and Jackie bubble

about dresses and flowers and food for the reception. Mike and Chris discuss reception halls and music and how expensive everything is. Then a voice cuts through it all.

"How lovely that you're getting married, Jackie," says Regina. "And Chris, too. On the same day, no less."

Same day? What's she talking about?

"But where are your grooms? Shouldn't they be here, too?"

Grooms? Is she serious? Doesn't she understand that Aunt Jackie and Chris are gay?

Everyone stares at her like they don't know what to say. How to explain it to her. Even Gigi seems confused.

"Mother," says Mike. "Jackie and Chris are marrying . . . um . . . *each other.*"

"What?" Regina's eyes practically bug out of her head. "That's not even legal, is it?"

Aunt Jackie snorts. I guess this isn't the first time she's heard it.

"Some places it is," says Chris. "It might not be recognized in Michigan—yet—but our friends and family—"

"And *us.* It's about us first and foremost." Jackie puts her arm around Chris and looks right at Regina. "We are publicly and formally committing to each other."

"What about children?" Regina folds her napkin and sets it next to her plate. "Don't you want children someday?"

"Excuse me?" Aunt Jackie snaps.

"*If* and *when* we decide to have children," Chris cuts in, "there are lots of choices out there."

"How about strawberry shortcake?" asks Mom. "The strawberries are locally grown and really delicious."

Nice going, Mom. Typical Suzy Galardi-Logan strategy: To avoid confrontation, offer food as a diversion.

"Won't all this be confusing for the child?" Regina won't let it go. "Two mothers and no father. What would the last name be? I just don't understand. It's just not *natural.*"

Jackie slams her hand on the table, startling everyone. "*You* don't have to understand. It's not about *you!*"

Chris is much calmer. "We believe that love—"

"You don't owe her an explanation, Chris. She's not confused. She's judgmental."

Chris shuts up, picks a cherry tomato off her plate, and pops it in her mouth. I do the same, except with a stray morsel of roast beef. I would go check on the kids, but I don't want to draw any attention to myself. Not even by getting up. I know it's awful, and I feel bad for them—it sucks to be judged—but part of me is glad the attention is off me.

Mom continues with her original strategy. She gets up and grabs bowls. Mike follows her. She puts shortcake in each one and ladles the sweet, juicy strawberries on top.

"I am not judgmental," says Regina. "There is a man in the salon where I get my hair done who is gay. I always say hello to him." Aunt Jackie rolls her eyes.

Mike adds the finishing touches of whipped cream and a spoon for each bowl. They place one in front of each person, as if the sight of dessert will cause instant harmony. I know better, but the strawberries smell wonderful.

Jackie shrugs. "I give up."

"Shortcake." Mom puts her face right into Jackie's, as if to say, *Drop it and eat.*

"No thanks." Jackie stands up. "I've lost my appetite."

I wish I lost my appetite when I got upset.

When Mike serves Regina, she pulls him into the conversation. "What do you think, Michael? Is this the kind of influence you want on *your* children?"

"Yes, *Michael*," says Aunt Jackie sarcastically. "What do you think? What about the judgmental influence on your children?"

Just what I was afraid of.

"Well," says Mike, sitting down. "I, uh, love you both and . . ." He spoons strawberries and whipped cream into his mouth.

"And what?" asks Regina.

He swallows. "And I'm happy to have all of you in my children's lives. *All* of you."

Always the politician—schmooze everyone and avoid a real stand.

Regina slowly and deliberately gets up, pushes in her chair, and huffs out of the room and up the stairs, leaving her dessert behind.

"That woman!" says Jackie through gritted teeth. "You're a saint to put up with her."

Mom's eyes get big and she nods toward Mike, signaling to Jackie to tone it down. Regina is, after all, his mother. "So, does Mom know yet? And Doug?"

"Not yet. Mom's Up North with her fat-ass friends." Jackie imitates Gram, and all of us laugh, including Chris, who usually tells Aunt Jackie to be nice. "I'll tell her when she gets back, and Doug later tonight."

"Ann and I will have to go dress shopping tomorrow," says Mom. "There's no time to waste. Want to come, too, Jack?"

"I can't. Family dinner at Chris's dad's," she says. "Whatever you and Ann decide will be fine. I trust you. I'll match the ribbon in the flowers to your dresses."

More shopping! With Mom in control of everything. Tomorrow. My gut flutters. Visions of the last time I tried on a dress flash through my mind. If I'm going to look good at Aunt Jackie's wedding, I'll need to lose forty-five pounds. By the middle of August.

8

A COUPLE OF HOURS LATER, AUNT JACKIE AND Chris leave. I just want to veg out in my room, but Mom makes me help clean up the kitchen. Maybe moving will speed up the digestive process. Mike takes the twins for a bike ride while Regina snores upstairs.

"Where do you think we should start?" Mom stacks plates on the counter. "The bridal shop or Keehn's formal department? We might even find a discounted prom dress this time of year."

"I don't know." I scrape leftover food into the garbage. I know which plate is mine. The clean one.

"What do you think of yellow or maybe a spring green?" Mom suggests colors that look good on her, not me.

I say nothing. The thought of trying on any dress at this weight nauseates me. I load the silverware into the dishwasher.

"Ann?" Mom is in my face. "What's wrong?"

"Nothing."

"Then why do you look like you're about to cry? Aren't you happy for Jackie and Chris?"

"Yes, of course," I say.

"Then what's the matter?"

"I just don't want to go shopping." I keep loading the dishwasher, so I don't have to look at her.

"What do you mean?" she asks.

"I don't know." I'm struck with self-consciousness. How can I tell her that I want to go on another diet? That I need to lose weight before the wedding. Any idiot can see that if you don't want to be fat, you shouldn't eat so much. You should move more. Any idiot could see that. Any idiot is smarter than me.

Mom always wants to help, but she doesn't get it. It was one thing when I wanted a push to get me motivated. That was hypothetical. That was *want*. This—the wedding—is real. This is *need*. This is way scarier. I can't talk about it. Not yet. Instead I wipe down the table. And put the placemats away.

"Ann, we'll need to get dresses," says Mom. "The wedding is just a couple months away. Is something wrong?"

"No!" I snap, not meaning to. "Can we just go in a couple weeks? Maybe three?" By then, I should have lost some weight and maybe even a dress size. A little time—a few weeks, tops—is all I need.

"That's really pushing it if we need to have the dresses altered, but I guess so. Will you tell me why?"

Before I can tell her that I'd rather not, Regina appears. "Oh!" She sounds surprised. "You're not making supper?"

"We just had a big dinner a few hours ago," says Mom, "so I didn't plan to make anything. Maybe some popcorn later or something. Why? Are you hungry?"

Regina always does this. Mom slaves over a big meal that she hardly touches, and then, once everything is cleaned up, she wants something else. "Just a bit. Maybe a ham sandwich. Do you have any coleslaw?"

"No, I don't," says Mom patiently. "How about some chips?"

"Potato chips are so salty and fattening," she says. "How about a pickle? And real mayo on the sandwich. Not that fake diet stuff you always have. Do you have any pie?"

She can't eat chips because they're salty and fattening, but pickles, mayo, and pie are okay?

"No pie, but I have some strawberry shortcake left."

"I don't care for strawberries. That's fine, though," she says, although it's clearly not. "I'll take my sandwich in the other room with my magazine. Oh, and a glass of ginger ale. No ice." And she practically sweeps out of the room. Queen Regina has spoken.

I sit at the table and text Cassie. *Hey. Regina is here. OMG. Nothing has changed. What are you doing tonight?*

Mike and the twins get home while Mom is making Regina's sandwich. She yanks him into the laundry room off the kitchen, closes the door, and gives him an earful. I can't hear the words, but I can hear her ranting. In a few minutes, he comes out, pours a glass of ginger ale, and delivers the plate and glass to the queen's throne.

Mom heads upstairs and is back down in seconds with her running clothes on. She's out the door without saying a word.

Mike picks up the remote and flips through the stations. I see that the Secrets 2 Success infomercial is on again. On my way to my room to get my laptop, I hear Regina say, "I just don't understand how those people could let themselves get so fat in the first place."

I move a pile of clothes from my bed to the chair in the corner. There is already a bunch of clothes in the chair, so I have to adjust the balance to keep the whole heap from sliding to the floor. Moving the pile unearths some M&M's wrappers, so I shove them under my bed.

First, I check Facebook. Tony has a new profile pic. He's wearing a Laker tee and holding something. Is that a football? He doesn't play football. Not since seventh grade, anyway.

One summer Nate and Naomi spent a couple of weeks with their dad, so Dad and Nancy took Tony and me to Michigan Adventure for a weekend. Just the four of us. I was thrilled. Dad rode roller coasters and bought us hot dogs and cotton candy. But all he talked about was golf and hockey and football, and in the hotel room, all he watched was sports.

When school started, Tony joined the middle school football team. He played four games, and Dad didn't come to any of them. So he quit.

I overheard Uncle Doug call Dad a dickhead when Mom told him about it. *He is not!* I defended Dad. *He's just busy.* I believed Dad would have come, if only Tony had stuck it out a while longer.

Mom shot Uncle Doug a dagger stare, and he apologized. But I knew he didn't mean it. After that, I noticed that Dad rarely missed one of Nate's hockey games or Naomi's gymnastics meets. I always wondered if he wanted to go or if Nancy made him. I bet Tony noticed, too, but we never talked about it.

I "like" Tony's picture just to remind him that I still exist. I try not to "like" too much, though, because I'm afraid he'll delete or block me. He probably filters me already because the last thing I can see, besides the new pic, is from April. Unless he just doesn't post much. I don't know. I don't know anything about him anymore.

I check my phone. Cassie hasn't texted back.

Then I click on the S2S website and read over the testimonials, including Natalie S.'s. I compare their starting weights with mine, how much weight they lost, and how long it took. They all lost almost ten pounds the first week. I should be able to do that, too. Then I can go dress shopping and get a feel for the sizes. After that, I should be able to lose about two or three pounds a week. That's another twenty or thirty pounds. I might not lose quite forty-five by the wedding but for sure by the time school starts in the fall.

This time is going to be different. I won't be able to screw it up. The plan says to just eat the pre-packaged meals as directed, take the supplements, follow the exercise program, and lose. Idiotproof. I am pumped. No more misery. I'll look good for Aunt Jackie's wedding. People will tell me how proud they are of me or how they wish they had the willpower to stick to a diet program like I do. People at school will want to talk to me, too. They'll want me to go to dances, and I'll go because I won't be embarrassed anymore.

The clothes heap in the chair starts to slide. I ignore it. The pictures of the food look good—pizza, panini, lasagna, and chocolaty protein bars. I get to eat cereal and veggie chips and pudding. Heck, I'll be eating all day. Why didn't I do this before?

I fish around in my drawer and find my debit card. A Napanelli's receipt is wrapped around it. Ironic. The last time I used this card was to order pizza that is probably still on my hips. Now I'm using it to buy pizza that'll take *that* pizza off.

It'll drain practically every cent from my account, but it'll be worth it. I'll get a job and put it all back. After I place my order, though.

The clothes heap falls to the floor. I make a mental note that that pile is clean and move on.

I try ordering online. I type in all my information five different times and click NEXT, but it keeps taking me back to the home page. Something must be screwy with their site. I'm going to have to order over the phone.

Why couldn't I just text it in? I hate talking to people. What if they ask me something I don't know the answer to, and I sound like an idiot? I'm not used to ordering things or talking on the phone. I take a deep breath and dial.

"Welcome to the first step in the rest of your life—the Secrets 2 Success Weight Loss System," a recording croons. "A revolutionary new program designed uniquely for you. Please hold the line and one of our representatives will be with you shortly." I listen to upbeat techno music while I wait. Good. Time to calm down and think about what I want to say.

"Thank you for holding. Your call is important to us. We are experiencing usually high call volume. Please continue to hold. We will be with you shortly. This call may be recorded for training purposes. Be sure to ask your operator about our auto-ship program and never have to worry about running out of S2S food or Super Supplements. They'll all ship right to your door, automatically! Please have your credit card ready."

More techno music. More waiting.

A very enthusiastic voice breaks in. "Hi, I'm Brianna." I picture her toothpick-size and tan, with a blonde ponytail, glittery eye shadow, and tons of mascara. "Are you ready to take the first step in the rest of your life?"

"Sure."

"Great!" she says. "Visa, MasterCard, Discover, or American Express?"

"Brianna," I ask, trying to sound more upbeat, "have you tried S2S yourself?"

"Um . . . well . . ."

Just as I thought. Toothpick. She's probably never even met Natalie S.

"Never mind," I say, letting her off the hook. "My card is a debit MasterCard."

"Great!"

I can't believe I'm actually doing this. My voice shakes as I give her my information. She reads it all back to me for verification. Then she asks if I want to sign up for auto-ship. "Only $319.99 a month! That's 25% off the buy-as-you-go price." *Three hundred and twenty bucks a month?* I can't afford that! I thought the *whole system* was eighty bucks. She says that's the introductory rate—for the first two weeks—just to get started. Then the food is about ten dollars a day and supplements are about twenty a month, but only if you auto-ship. Otherwise, it's even more. Holy guacamole! I *am* going to need to get a job. And fast. This whole thing is going to cost about a grand! Should I even do it at all?

What are my options? I picture myself standing next to Mom and Aunt Jackie at the wedding looking like a satiny sectional, decorative pillows and all. I have to do something.

"Hello?" asks Brianna. "Shall I put you down for auto-ship? You can cancel at any time. And you get an extra week's worth of food for free, just for signing up."

"Um . . ." I say. I'm nervous. I don't know what to do. Just like I was afraid of. *Idiot!* If I say no, I'll have to pay another twenty-five percent when I order more food. But if I say yes and can't get a job, there won't be money in my account. I think you can go to jail for that sort of thing. But she said I can cancel at any time.

"How easy is it to cancel?" I ask.

"You just log on to your account on our website and uncheck the auto-ship box," she bubbles. "It's that simple."

"I don't have an account, though."

"All the instructions for creating an account and accessing our online community are included in your welcome packet."

"Okay," I say. "Sign me up." I exhale. All or nothing. While I'm at it I even upgrade to express delivery. I should have my S2S system by Tuesday or Wednesday.

Immediately after I hang up, I regret calling.

Is this plan really doable?

According to *Slimmer You*, the ideal weight range for my height is 124-138 pounds. I'd be happy with 140. I think. The last time I was 140 was in middle school.

At my annual physical a couple of weeks ago I was exactly 185. The stupid wench nurse said it out loud as she wrote it down. Good thing Mom wasn't there.

Can I really lose forty-five pounds by the wedding?

Or is it going to be another entry on my long list of failures?

Then I think of Mom. Once she realizes I'm trying to lose weight again, she'll be giddy and supportive and talk about it constantly. She'll watch me even closer than she usually does. I can't take that. I decide to keep this program a secret. I don't care that *Slimmer You* says that support is essential to weight loss. They have never met my mother.

9

I NEED A JOB. NOW. BEFORE THE S2S PEOPLE
auto-bill me. I start at the Snapz! website because I know it so well.
It takes over an hour to apply because I have to fill out a personality test. Seriously. A personality test. Two hundred and twelve
questions like *How do you react when people criticize you?* Since
Eating a half-gallon of ice cream isn't one of the options, I go with
I keep it inside and worry. I figure that is more desirable than *I yell
and throw things.*

Then I check local job listings at *The Citizen Patriot.* There isn't
much out there for someone still in high school. I search other
mall store websites and apply at The Gap, Claire's, and Bath & Body
Works.

I even apply at Mondo Burger. They are partly to blame for my
fat ass, after all, being so beefy and cheesy and pickly and special
saucy. Just looking at the site makes me want a Mondo Burger so
bad! Working there might not be such a great idea.

I Google "jobs Jackson, MI." Some of the ads are the same as
The Cit Pat, and everyone still wants a degree or experience. While

I'm reading the job requirements for a Product Media Specialist and not understanding half of it, I get a text from Cassie. *pool party. my house. now. wanna come?*

Huh? Cassie doesn't have a pool. I doubt one would even fit in her yard. I text back: *???* To which she replies: *just get over here!!! LOL*

It's almost nine o'clock, but Cassie's is just three houses away. Mom won't mind. *K. be right there.*

"You spending the night?" Mom asks, much too hopefully. She's huffing away on the elliptical in the basement while Mike, Regina, and the twins watch cartoons on Nick Jr.

"Don't think so." Cassie and I used to be practically joined at the hip during summer vacation. The question our mothers asked was not *Are you spending the night*, but *Will you be here or there tonight?* Maybe Cassie invited me over because summer is Ann-and-Cassie time, no matter which school we go to. Maybe I'll end up sleeping over. Halfway up the stairs, I call back. "If I do, I'll text you."

From the front walk, I hear laughing and loud music, so I head around back. "Annie!" Cassie screams and runs over to me, slipping on the wet patio but recovering before she falls. *Annie?* She hugs me, which I don't think she's done since we were twelve, and she smells like beer. "Hope you brought your suit." She flings her arm up like a game show model unveiling a new car.

On the lawn just off the patio sits a tiny blue plastic kiddie pool with a garden hose draped over the side. Three of Cassie's tennis friends are sitting in folding chairs around it with their feet soaking. All of them are in bikinis, and I'm the fattest one here. Cassie, whose arms and legs are even longer, leaner, and tanner than usual—tennis season always puts her in good shape for summer—

steps into the middle of the pool and plops on her ass, splashing the other girls. Laughter erupts.

"Have a seat." Cassie waves at the only empty chair. "You guys remember Ann, right? She's my bestest friend." She smiles big and it reminds me of when we were younger, when she introduced me as her bestest friend—to new kids at school, to people we'd meet camping, to everyone. Like we were a package deal.

I've met Cassie's new friends a couple of times this past school year. I don't really know them, but after her birthday party last November, they added me on Facebook. Except for my family, Cassie introduced me to pretty much every one of my two hundred "friends."

"Cute flip-flops," says Grace. "Snapz!, right?"

I smile and nod. "Where did you get the pool, Cass?"

"Funny story." Cassie yanks the hair tie from her ponytail and flings it at one of the girls. Her dark auburn hair cascades down her shoulders like she's in a shampoo commercial. "Hey, Bri, toss me a beer, will ya?"

As Bri reaches into the cooler next to her, Cassie says, "Maddy's cousin's grad party was today. Stephanie Rogers—you know her?" I shake my head.

"You want a beer, Ann?" Bri tosses a can to Cassie, and she pops it open.

"No thanks."

"Why not?" Cassie says. "You on a diet again or something?"

My face burns. Why would Cassie say that? She *knows* how sensitive I am about my diets. Especially since they clearly haven't worked. Most especially in front of people I hardly know. Nobody says a word—least of all, me.

"What? Did I say something wrong? It's true." She pauses between each sentence, obviously waiting for me to agree with her and tell her it's fine. I don't. I just stare at her, hoping she gets the point and shuts up. She doesn't. "You go on a lot of diets. Nothing to be ashamed of. Right, Grace?" Is that supposed to be a dig at Grace, too?

There is a *very* awkward silence.

After a moment, Grace, who has the most gorgeous red hair I've ever seen, says, "Okay, well, back to the story."

Cassie splashes in the pool totally oblivious of her bitchiness, as usual. Also, as usual, nobody calls her on it. "Yeah, yeah, right. Anyway. Stephanie's mom filled this pool with ice and put water bottles, pop, and beer in it. Maddy here"—Cassie pokes Maddy's leg—"and Bri volunteered to refill it as needed. Aren't they helpful?" Maddy poses and smiles.

"Marvelous job, ladies." Grace claps. "Marvelous!" *God, drunk people are annoying.*

"And for every case of beer we opened," Bri continued, "we smuggled four—"

"Or five—" says Maddy.

"Or six beers into this cooler for ourselves."

"But how did you end up with the pool?" I ask.

"Once the party wrapped up, Steph's mom was going to throw it away." Cassie takes a swig and then belches. "Can you believe it? She said she only bought it for the party and had no place to keep it. So, I said we'd take it."

"Getting it home on top of Cassie's Focus was the best part," says Grace. "We threw it on the roof and held it down as she drove home. It only fell off once!" They all laugh.

As Maddy pops open another beer, I ask, "Cassie, aren't your parents home?"

"Nope. They're Up North until Sunday night for some Boy Scout jamboree thing with Carter." Carter is Cassie's younger brother. "Pool party all weekend, baby!"

"Guess who came into work today?" Grace says.

"Who?"

"Coach Todd. With his girlfriend!" Great! They're talking about people I don't know. This is just like lunch at school. Why am I even here?

"He has a *girlfriend*?"

"Yeah, and she's really pretty. So much for all your flirting, Cassie. He's taken."

"Bummer," she says. "But who says that's going to stop me?" The other girls laugh and tell her she's "so bad." She smirks and tosses back her hair.

"Where do you work?" I ask Grace.

"Bath and Body Works."

Ooh! Maybe she'll put in a good word for me. "I just applied there. Are they hiring?"

"No. We have so many people working there that I hardly get any hours as it is, and the manager says she gets dozens of apps a day that she just ignores. Sorry."

"It's okay." But it doesn't feel okay. What if I can't get a job?

"I've been looking since May," says Maddy. "There's nothing out there. Nothing good, anyway."

"You could always work at Mondo Burger," says Cassie. *Is she talking to Maddy or me?*

"Yeah. You want fries with that?" Maddy mocks. "Can you see me in that ugly uniform? No way!"

"I love this song!" Bri cranks up the iPhone dock to the point of distortion, jumps in the pool with Cassie, and pulls her to her feet. "Dance party! Come on, you guys!"

Grace and Maddy hop in. Since the pool is only about two feet across, they're bumping into each other as they wiggle and shake. Water sloshes all over the patio.

"Come on in, Ann," calls Bri, "the more the merrier!"

"Yeah." Cassie pushes Bri and Maddy aside to clear a spot. "We'll make room."

I'm not about to squeeze myself into that tiny pool with them. Especially not to jiggle on purpose. No way.

"I'm good, thanks." I wave. "I'm going to head home. Regina's in town, and I don't want to wake her by coming in too late."

"Yeah, okay." Cassie dismisses me and continues to dance. Grace waves, but Bri and Maddy don't even notice.

The house is dead quiet when I get home, and I feel strangely empty. Like I have nothing to do except wait. For the S2S system to arrive. For someone to call me for an interview. For my life to begin. All this waiting stresses me out. I head to the kitchen and scarf down another bowl of strawberry shortcake. Only a little whipped cream, though.

10

REGINA HOGS THE UPSTAIRS BATHROOM THE NEXT morning. I swear I could have finished my entire eleventh-grade summer reading list while she was in there. It probably takes a lot of effort to disguise those devil horns and fill in those old lady wrinkles.

I join the family for breakfast. Mike scrolls through his news downloads at one end of the table, and Mom folds towels at the other. The twins share a chair and some Play-Doh; across from them, I search for jobs on my phone.

Regina appears, looking embalmed—as if she used spackle for foundation—and somewhat confused. Although, after staring for an inappropriately long time, I realize it's because her eyebrows are drawn on unevenly.

"What's the matter, Mother?" asks Mike.

"I thought there'd be breakfast before I hit the road," she whines. "I really didn't want to stop until I got to Carol's. You know how the midday traffic near Chicago is."

"I had Frosty Nuggets, Grammy," says Libby. "They're yummy."

"*Frosty Nuggets* are *not* breakfast, Liberty," scolds Regina.

"Let's go this route, then." Mom is snippier this morning. I know that her fuse is only so long. I just hope I'm out of range when she explodes. "What would you like?"

"An omelet would be nice," she says, "but don't go to any trouble for me. Mike, wouldn't you want one, too?"

Not even looking up from his phone, Mike lifts his coffee mug. "All I need is the nectar of the gods."

"Nonsense! Everyone should have a good breakfast. Suzanne, don't you feed your family a decent breakfast, at least on *Sunday* mornings?"

Mom opens the fridge, pulls out a carton of eggs, and slams the door.

"Suzy does a great job feeding us, Mother," says Mike. "We're just not that hungry in the morning. Especially after such a large dinner last night." He grins in Mom's direction, probably thinking he deserves a medal for taking her side.

Mom pulls out a mixing bowl and slams the cupboard. And the drawer. She says nothing, but her point is clear: this was not what she had planned.

"Mommy's loud," says Judd, using his whole body to work his plastic rolling pin.

"You have to be loud when you cook." Libby slaps her dough with both hands. "That's the rules."

"Well, I'd better get packed," says Regina in a sing-song voice. Like she has no idea the havoc she's causing.

As soon as she's up the stairs, Mom lays into Mike. "How many times do I have to mess up the kitchen today? I thought you said she'd be gone by now. She's not." All through clenched teeth. Quiet enough not to travel upstairs, but forceful enough for him to get the point. "I have things to do today, *Michael* . . ." She continues ranting as she chops, beats, and flips. By the time Regina comes downstairs with her suitcase, there's a full breakfast ready for her on the table.

"Well, I'm off," sings Regina.

"Mother, your breakfast is ready," says Mike.

"Oh, I don't have time, dear," she says. "Carol is expecting me."

Mom's mouth falls open and fire blazes in her eyes.

"Suzy put a lot into it," says Mike. "The least you can do is eat it."

"*You'll* eat it, won't you?" she says. "I really don't have time. Besides, it's nearly eleven o'clock now. Nearly lunchtime. But a ham sandwich for the road would be nice."

Mom grabs her keys and leaves, slamming the garage door behind her.

"Hmmm," Regina says. "What's the matter with her? Such a display over a sandwich."

"I'll make it, Mother." Mike pulls the ham and mustard out of the fridge. "But honestly, would it have killed you to eat the omelet you asked for?"

I could swear she has a look of triumph on her face. "It took too long, and I'm pressed for time."

Mike slices the ham, pulls out the mustard, and slaps together a sandwich. No cheese. No lettuce. No frills. Then he folds a paper towel around it and sets it on her suitcase by the door. Gigi follows, but once she sees Regina, she backs up and runs upstairs.

"Thank you, dear." Then she pulls a camera from her purse and announces, "Picture time!"

"Pictures? Thought you were pressed for time," snaps Mike. Just what I was thinking.

"There's always time for pictures," she says. "Gather 'round, family!" She doesn't ask where Mom is.

The twins immediately hop down, flank Mike in front of the fireplace, and grin. They love cameras. I stay right where I am, pretending I didn't hear anything.

"Come on, Ann," says Regina. "We need you, too."

I hate getting my picture taken. They always make me look even fatter than I am. But there is something about the words *we need you, too* that wins me over. I walk over and stand behind Libby. Maybe she can shield my gut. Part of it, anyway. I plaster on my fake smile.

Regina laughs. "Oh, no, dear, I need you to *take* the picture." Laughs like my being in the picture is the most preposterous thing she's ever heard.

"And then *I'll* take one of you, the twins, *and Ann*, right, Mother?" says Mike.

I slink over and take the camera from her, smile wiped clean.

"If that's what you want, dear. Here's the button," she instructs. "Just point and click." Then she stands where I was just seconds ago. She puts one arm around Mike's shoulders and her other hand on Libby's. She smiles big. A stupid, toothy, witchy grin.

I hold up the camera and snap the picture. No *say cheese*, no 1-2-3, nothing. Just snap. I'm not even sure if everyone was in the frame. I don't care. Maybe I cut Regina's head off. If only I could do it for real.

"Now take one of me and Ann, Grammy," says Libby.

"And me, too," says Judd.

"Maybe next time, children," she says lightly. "I need to be going."

"Mother? Surely, you have time for one more. *There's always time for pictures*, remember?" Mike's tone is insistent, icy.

Regina stands and fidgets like Gigi while he takes a picture of us. I don't smile. Then she leans down to Libby and taps her cheek. "Now give Grammy a kiss."

Libby refuses and pouts. She wants more pictures.

"Come on, Liberty," she coaxes.

Don't do it, Lib. Don't let her manipulate you.

Then Mike whispers something in Libby's ear. She perks up and runs over and gives Regina a quick peck. Judd does, too.

After she leaves, Libby heads for the cookie jar. Mike gives the twins an Oreo each. He's mastered Mom's parenting control technique: bribery with food. Works every time.

Speaking of food, Regina's omelet sits on the table, untouched. A piece of ham peeks out. I pop it in my mouth. It's cold, but really good. I break off a piece of egg and eat it. The next thing I know I'm picking up the fork and taking a bite. Then another.

Mom comes through the garage door.

"Mommy's home," announces Judd.

"Perfect timing," says Mike. "Mother just left."

"I know," says Mom. "I heard her. I got in the van, ready to peel out of here when I realized that her car was behind mine. There was no way I was going to ask her to move it, and ramming it with our van wasn't an option. But don't think I didn't entertain the idea! So I sat in the garage and listened to NPR. Did you know that the average American consumes over one hundred and sixty pounds of sugar a year? That's over thirty-two five-pound bags of sugar *each*!"

Mike crosses the kitchen and hugs her. "You're the best wife anyone could ask for," he says. "Thank you for not killing my mother."

"Damn straight," says Mom. "And you're welcome. I could have easily, you know, and no court would convict me."

"I know," he says.

Then Mom sees me. "God, Antoinette! Do something besides eat, will you?"

Boom! Shrapnel to the face. I stop mid-chew. The soft egg and cheese seem to expand in my mouth, and I want to spit it out. But there is no place for it to go. So I swallow. It has a hard time getting past the lump in my throat, but I force it. Just like me in this house. In this family. In my life. Forced down the throats of those who are already full.

11

THREE DAYS LATER, I'M POLISHING MY TOES SPARkly fuchsia and sitting in front of the TV. Just Gigi and me. Mom and Mike are at work, and the twins are at day care. Part of me wishes I could babysit them, since I really need the money, but if Mom let me do that, Judd and Libby wouldn't have a guaranteed spot at Donna's Day Care come fall. The other part of me is glad I'm not tethered to them all summer, especially if I get another job.

I know I shouldn't be waiting around. I should be proactive and exercise or start eating better, but it'll be easier when my S2S system gets here. But then there's the feeling that I'd better eat all the crap I can now, because once I start on S2S there'll be no more real food for a long time. It's a guiltless procrastination excuse for both eating and not exercising. As I finish off the last night's leftover Napanelli's pizza and watch *Everybody Loves Raymond* reruns, I soothe myself by saying, *It's okay. Everything is going to change once the S2S system gets here.*

Is this really going to work? After all, nothing has in the past. Well, other things have worked, but I never stuck with them. They helped me get the weight off, or at least some of it, but none of them have been doable long term. So how is S2S any different? Am I really going to fork out three hundred bucks a month for food for the rest of my life?

I pore over the website. According to the testimonials and the dietician who designed the program, these pre-portioned meals will re-train my brain for what portions are really supposed to look like so that when I get weaned back onto "real" lasagna, I'll understand portion control, which (according to *Slimmer You*) is the key to sustaining weight loss.

I hope they're right. But today I'm skeptical. Today I feel dumpy. I have to do something.

Not actual exercise, though. I wouldn't want to get ahead of myself. No. I decide to prepare for my job interviews. I don't actually have any yet, but I'm convinced that if I'm prepared, I'll have a shot.

I bring my laptop back to the couch and start with the Snapz! website since that would be my dream job. I learn the names of all the different collections—SoHo, Cali, Zany, Sick, and Retro—and brush up on translating sizing from other popular stores. Is it a coincidence that I get a call from the Snapz! assistant manager while I'm on their website? I think not.

"Can you come in tomorrow at ten A.M.?" she asks.

"Yes." I say nervously.

"Great! You'll be meeting with Ryann."

"Thank you." I am so excited that as soon as I hang up the phone, I whoop and holler and dance around. Gigi joins in. She likes to dance. I know poodles are smart, but ours actually has some killer moves.

"Going to Snapz! tomorrow," I sing. "Gonna get me a really cool job. Uh-huh."

While I'm dancing around like an idiot, I see something through the window next to the front door. A guy in a brown outfit. How long has he been there? Did he knock? I open the door as he's putting the package on the porch. Gigi barks her head off. *Yeah, now you bark. Where were you when I could have used a warning? Huh?*

"Oh, hi." He hands it to me. "I didn't think anyone was home. Have a nice day."

My S2S system is here! My S2S system is here! More singing. More dancing.

I rip open the box and unload all the stuff—booklets and packets and smaller boxes and frozen entrées packed in dry ice and supplements and two DVDs and a big rubber exercise band. How can I hide all this from Mom? I stash the frozen stuff in the freezer in the garage, under the crystallized fish sticks. The rest will fit under my bed in the box.

But first I read through everything. This is going to be a cinch. I just follow the plan: cereal or a shake for breakfast, an energy bar mid-morning, soup (from a packet) and salad for lunch, a piece of fruit or veggie chips for an afternoon snack, and a frozen entrée and salad for dinner. Then do the workout DVD three times a week. Easy breezy.

What if Cassie wants to go for a Mondo Burger? Or ice cream? I prep some excuses, learned from Mom, the master. *I'm so full; I ate a big breakfast.* Or I could order stuff, but not eat it. Yeah, right.

For days there's been nothing but reruns on TV, a couple of easy summer reads, and general boredom. Then everything happens at once. My new eating and exercise plan *and* a job prospect. My new life! My new-and-improved self begins today! Well, maybe not today. Today is half over.

Better to start fresh tomorrow.

12

MY BLACK DRESS SHOES *SQUEAK, SQUEAK, squeak* on the mall floor. The few people there at ten o'clock on a Wednesday morning glance at me and then away. I know what they're thinking. They're glad *their* shoes aren't squeaking. How embarrassing! Finally they stop when I enter the carpeted store.

Snapz!

I'm shaky, and my heart is racing. I'm not sure if it's just nerves or the S2S nutritional supplement pill I took this morning.

"Hi!" A perfect size negative-something continues to fold tank tops. "Welcome to Snapz! Can I help you find something?"

"Um, yeah," I say. "Ryann. I have an appointment with him for an interview."

She giggles. "*She's* in the back."

My face burns. Great. I've only just walked into the store and already stuck my foot in my mouth.

I stand near the door to "the back." Should I go in? Or wait for her? Should I ask the girl to get her for me? Shouldn't she just go get her? After all, she knows why I'm here. My face feels hotter, redder by the second.

I look around at all the clothes. If only I could wear them. I fantasize about when I lose the forty-five pounds. Maybe I'll do my back-to-school shopping here. I make mental notes of all the shirts I would want to try on. I visualize myself in them, just like *Slimmer You* says to. Maybe I'll do the workout DVD four times a week to hurry it along.

Suddenly the door opens and there's a tall woman with very short, spiky hair with a phone to her ear. "Yeah," she says. If she sees me, she makes no acknowledgement. I wait. "I know. Right." She grabs some paper from under the counter and heads back toward the door. Then she turns to me and mouths, "Are you Ann?"

I nod and hope I don't look as terrified as I feel.

She motions for me to follow her, all the while still on the phone.

The office is tiny—pretty much a closet within a storage room. A desk, two folding chairs, and a file cabinet with a printer on it. I'm not sure what I expected—probably not boas and sequined tops draped on funky leather couches and framed artsy fashion pics on the wall—but something much more chic than this. It smells like the custodial mop closet at school.

I sit in a folding chair, which is not nearly as sturdy as it looks. I'm afraid to fidget too much. What if it falls to pieces like Baby Bear's chair underneath Goldilocks' gigantic butt? I shift my weight onto my feet as much as possible. I try to relax, but I'm sure that I look constipated instead.

Finally the woman says, "Hey, I have to go . . . yeah . . . okay . . . bye." She sets the phone down and reaches to shake my hand. "Hi, I'm Ryann."

73

I carefully lean forward and shake. "I'm Ann." That's all I should say, but, no, I keep talking. "But you already know that." I giggle. Giggle? I never giggle! "You're Ryann. A *woman*." *Duh!* "It makes sense. You know, since Snapz! *is* a woman's store." She smiles—close-mouthed, eyebrows raised.

Shut up, my brain tells my mouth. *Just shut up now.* My heart is still racing. But my mouth is even faster.

"At first, I thought you were a guy." Then I try to backtrack. "Not that you *look* like a guy." And end up making it worse. "Even though your hair *is* really short." I wish she'd say something, anything, and end my blathering, but she doesn't. "I like your hair. I mean, it's super cute. It's just Ryann is usually a guy's name." More giggling. "I bet you get that all the time."

Ryann stares and nods slowly, as if she's thinking all this random stuff is crazy. Maybe because it is. I would slap myself, but then I'd look crazier.

Shut up! Please just shut up now. Finally my mouth listens to my brain.

I shift in my seat. The rickety chair creaks. Or, should I say, moans?

After an awkward silence, Ryann says, "Okay, then . . ."

She asks about my schedule—open—and my experience—none. I will myself to listen and answer confidently and professionally, but my mind keeps repeating how stupid I am. How I don't belong here. How I should leave and never set foot in the mall again. How I'm insensitive and should publicly apologize to everyone with a gender-neutral name.

We talk about my classes next year and my favorite places to shop. That's when she says, "We expect our employees to wear our

74

clothes. They're our best advertisers. If customers come into the store and see our competitors' clothes, what message does that send?"

Oh God. This hadn't occurred to me. Of course. It makes sense—the problem is that I can't do it. Yet. I do not want to say this out loud and admit that I am a cow. It's obvious. She's not blind.

Then I wonder if that thought was insensitive to blind people. And cows.

"We give employees a ten percent discount and allow up to one hundred dollars' credit per two-week pay period for store merchandise," she says, "which is deducted from your paycheck. One of our employees hasn't actually gotten a check yet." She laughs.

I smile. Not a real smile. One of those obligatory kinds of smiles. Why is she even bothering to interview me?

"I have a few more applicants." She stands and holds out her hand again. "You'll hear from me within the week if we're hiring you."

I stand and shake her hand. I guess that is my cue to go. "Thanks," I say.

I get out of there before I can say anything else stupid.

13

BEFORE I LEAVE THE MALL, I STOP AT THE TWISTED
Pretzel. It's down an entrance hall, not the food court, along with
the Orange Bowl, which sells smoothies that are higher in calories
than a large Mondo shake, and Grandma Lolly's Cookies.

I'm still kind of shaky and wonder if I should eat something.

My usual order of a giant pretzel with nacho cheese is not on
the S2S plan. Meal one—breakfast—was a tiny single-serving box
of cereal that tasted like Cheerios rolled in twigs. Up next is the
Belly Buster Bar. I glance at it as I pull out my wallet. Somebody's
spare tire belly with a big red X over it is pictured on the wrapper.
(Who'd ever want to be *that* model?)

Nacho cheese—creamy, kind of spicy, and soothing—is screaming my name. I need soothing after the morning I just had. Then
an excerpt from *Slimmer You* screams louder. "An ounce of willpower can battle a pound of fat." Then another, "Nothing tastes as
good as health and fitness feels." A one-two punch in the battle of
the bulge. I am empowered. But it's a baby-size empowerment. I

know it could fizzle any second—just a whiff of nacho cheese could do it.

I order quickly. "Medium Diet Coke, please."

Whew! I made it. Success feels good.

Raynee Gilbert takes my order. She is one of the Knee girls, with her friends Mela*nie*, Tiffa*ny*, and Court*ney*. In middle school they wore skirts and drew faces and words on their knees, usually things nobody understood but themselves. That eventually stopped, but they're still tight, and everyone still calls them the Knees.

I have been casual friends with most of them at one time or another, but I have never been to any of their houses. Cassie and I used to hang out with them sometimes, too. But that was because of Cassie.

"Hey, Ann." Raynee scoops ice into a paper cup. "How's your summer going?" Right now, of course, she's in a uniform, but she usually pairs bright colors with animal prints or something equally wild. Like Gram, Raynee has her own eclectic style. I'm not really the zebra-print type. More like an elephant. Do they make elephant print clothes? I realize I'm wearing a grayish-silver shirt. I guess they do.

"Fine," I say. I don't elaborate. I think I've spewed enough about me already today.

She snaps on the plastic lid. "You're all dressed up. . . ." A question disguised as an observation.

"I had an interview at Snapz! this morning."

"That's cool. Courtney used to work there. She spent all her money on clothes, so her mom made her quit." She hands me the drink and a straw. "Good thing you didn't order nacho cheese. It's chunky today and I'm not sure why." She makes a disgusted face.

"I heard that can be a problem." I hand her a five-dollar bill. "Spending your paycheck at Snapz!, I mean, not chunky nacho cheese. I don't spend a lot of time discussing that."

She laughs one of those polite, one syllable I-got-your-joke kind of laughs. "Think you got the job?"

"Doubt it." I don't give details.

"That's too bad." She counts back my change. "You know, we're hiring here. If you're interested."

"I could be," I say. "Do I have to have nacho cheese skills?"

"No worries." She laughs. "It's easy."

I fill out an application before I leave.

The Twisted Pretzel isn't nearly as cool as Snapz!, but it's a job, and I can't afford to be picky. S2S will be auto-shipping soon. Even if I get hired today, it'll be at least a week—maybe longer—before I actually get any money. I can't bring myself to think about that right now, though. If I'm not going to avoid dieting anymore, I might as well put my procrastination skills to use somewhere.

14

I RIP INTO THE BELLY BUSTER BAR AS SOON AS I
get into the car. It's really small but chewy and fudgy and peanut buttery. I almost convince myself that it's like a Little Debbie
brownie as I wash down the vitamin aftertaste with Diet Coke.
But the belches I have for the next few hours taste as if it con-
tained bits of actual spare tire. I make a mental note to never eat
it with anything fizzy again.

Even after I'm home a while, I'm still jittery. A warning on
the S2S supplement bottle says, "Heart palpitations, headaches,
shakiness, and/or dizziness may occur. Discontinue use if experiencing any of these symptoms, and see a physician if symptoms
persist." Natalie S. didn't say anything about side effects. *All natural*, my ass. Gram was right. I toss them into the trash and opt for
a one-a-day multivitamin instead.

Undeterred, I start my first S2S lunch, which is as easy to make
as boiling water. In fact, it *is* boiling water, flavored like chicken
noodle soup. There is no actual chicken in it and only a few floaty
things that resemble noodles. It's not horrible. Unlike the "ranch

dressing" for my side salad, which is an odd consistency—thick, unnaturally white globs. I'm careful not to poke the globs too much with my fork because they kind of creep me out.

After I whisk skim milk into the S2S pudding packet and pop it in the fridge, I check Facebook. Tony's new profile pic has twenty-seven "likes." I click through his photos, stopping at the one of us at his graduation a year ago—about a week before the big blow up. He's in his cap and gown and has his arm around me in a head-lock. Smirking, of course. My face—fat and shiny red from laugh-ing so hard—is turned toward his, which is long and thin, like the rest of him. I was mortified when he made it his profile because it made me look like I had no neck, just chin. I made him change it. Now I wish I hadn't because all I see is a brother and sister clown-ing around—happy.

I decide to take a chance and message Tony. *Hey! Aunt Jackie and Chris are getting married, and I'm in the wedding. Wish you'd come home for it. Miss you. Ann, your sister, in case you forgot.*

I know he's pissed at Mom and Mike and Dad and Nancy, but I can't figure out why he's cut himself off from me, Gram, Aunt Jackie, and Uncle Doug, too. We haven't done anything to him. That I know of. Sometimes I worry that something has happened to him, but then I realize that if it did, Mom would hear, and he wouldn't be updating his pics on Facebook.

Then I plop in front of the TV. Gigi jumps into my lap. This is going to be a long summer.

The first thing I see is a Mondo Burger commercial: "Real beef, real fast. You know you want one."

"Yes, yes, I do," I say to the TV. Gigi looks at me and cocks her curly little black head. I pat it to assure her that I'm not as crazy as I seem. "Be gone, Mondo Burger." I change the channel imperiously. "You have no power here." Okay. Maybe I *am* a little crazy after all.

The next channel has a potato chip commercial. The women eating them have probably never really had a potato chip in their lives. They hold the chips to their mouths and smile.

Click.

A talk show where the host is a former supermodel. "Everyday people can look fashion fabulous with these budget-stretching glamour tips," she says directly to me. "Right after the break."

A diet yogurt commercial. A gorgeous, tall, blonde sucks down several yogurts and then looks embarrassed. Is showing an anorexic binging on food supposed to make it more appetizing? That S2S chocolate pudding I whipped up for dinner is calling my name.

Click.

Mascara commercial. More supermodels.

Click.

Shampoo commercial. Now the models are naked.

Click.

Even a foot fungus treatment commercial has a sexy doctor and patients in it.

I can't take it anymore!

I grab the S2S workout DVD and the exercise band that goes with it. It's only a forty-five-minute workout. That's less than a TV drama, and they go by fast. It's 1:11 now. I'll be done by 1:56.

The instructor, Tia, is thin and perky and blonde. If I didn't know better, I'd swear she was the one who took my order. She tells me to follow Robin for the lighter workout and Terri for higher intensity. "Okay," she sings. "Let's get started. Feet hip distance apart, relax the knees. . . ."

At first it's just a warm up. It feels nice. Shrugging my shoulders. Rolling my head from side to front to side to back and around again. Stretching. Right arm stretching up. Left arm up. Hold each stretch for eight counts. The clock says 1:17. Thirty-nine minutes left.

The twenty-minute cardio section starts out harmlessly enough. Step right, together, tap left toe. Step left, together, tap right toe. Step, together, tap. Step, together, tap. "Let's add some arms to this," says Tia. I do okay, but then she throws in a combination. Did she say step, grapevine, knee thrust, squat? Or grapevine, step, squat, knee thrust? Whatever she said, I do it wrong. I must look like a dork. Gigi leaves the room, clearly embarrassed.

Eventually I'm in synch with her. Sort of. I miss the first part of each set while I figure out what she's doing, but at least I finish with her. 1:21. Thirty-five minutes to go.

"Let's pick up the pace." Tia hops around like she's skiing down a black diamond slope in the Olympics. Pick up the pace? What was wrong with the pace we were doing?

Arms up. Leg out. Knee up. Push up. Squat down. Arms out. Leg up. I'm glad I closed the blinds, because if the neighbors saw me, they'd think I was having a seizure and call 9-1-1.

Then I notice Robin, behind Tia. Her arms are lower and so are her kicks. Her squats are more shallow. The "lighter intensity" workout. I follow Robin for a while and catch my breath. 1:23. Will this ever end?

By 1:26, I am barely moving. If Tia's and Terri's arms are over their heads and Robin's are shoulder-high, mine don't leave my sides. Tia is hopping and lunging. Robin is stepping and lunging. I am stepping and stepping. Sweat drips down my face and my spine like a water spout, and it's grossing me out.

By 1:32, I am sitting on the floor sipping water and watching Tia jog and squat, jog and squat, arms pumping and reaching. "Ooh, I'm really starting to feel it," she says. "How about you?"

"Felt it at 1:20, Tia." I sip more water. "Now I'm numb to all feeling."

Finally the floor work starts. I get the green exercise band, lie down, and follow along. It starts out with stretching again, and she moves slowly enough that I can keep up. Gigi comes back and licks my face. While I push her away, I miss the first few counts but manage to catch up. I stretch and cool down with them. "Arms up, now pull," says Tia. "Breathe. Pull it. Resist. Like you're pulling through water."

"I am pulling through water, Tia." I yank on the band, which is hooked on the bottom of my heel. "A river of smelly sweat."

If the neighbors *did* call 9-1-1 earlier, I'd hate for the rescue workers to barge through the door right now. They'd see my fat thighs high in the air, tangled in a green rubber band. *No*, I would try to assure them. *I'm just doing my new workout DVD.* They would look me up and down. At my fat. At my sweaty, red face. And say, *Are you sure?* Then I imagine one of the rescue workers saying, *Hey, aren't you the girl who was trapped in a Snapz! dress a couple weeks ago?*

I crack up. "Even my imagination continues to be embarrassing," I say, now with my butt in the air. "I think I've lost my mind."

Gigi watches from the couch. She seems to agree.

When we get to the "home stretch," as Tia calls it, I'm tired—

but, I realize, in a good way. I reach up for the ceiling and take a deep breath. Tia, Robin, and Terri clap and cheer when it's over. I know they don't know me, but it feels like they're on my side.

I head to the shower. Doing that DVD was way better than watching back-to-back reruns. I turn on the water and peel off my sweaty shorts and T-shirt. Dinner—just three hours away. Lasagna, salad, and chocolate pudding. I've earned it.

15

MOM, MIKE, AND THE KIDS DON'T GET HOME
until after five, so I decide to eat about 4:30 to avoid questions
about my food and the temptation to eat theirs. I tear open the
box and pop the tray in the microwave. Seven minutes to gooey,
cheesy heaven. I can hardly wait.

One good thing about Mom being so anal about food is that
we always have salad fixings in the house. Salad is her main dish,
and whatever she makes for everyone else is her side. I fill a plate
and choose the zesty Italian S2S dressing packet to top my lettuce,
tomato, cucumber, and fat-free shredded cheddar cheese alterna-
tive. The "cheese" looks kind of like the plastic pretend cheese from
Libby's play kitchen. It's probably made by the same company.

I smell something weird and try to figure out where it is coming from. "Gigi, did you roll in something outside?" She cocks her
head like she's listening and thinking.

The microwave still shows 2:38. I watch the timer—2:37, 2:36,
2:35—while I rip open the dressing package and watch it plop onto
my salad in a single gelatinous glob. It creeps me out even more

than the little Ranch globs from lunch. I try spreading it onto the lettuce. I read the ingredients. The only words I recognize are vinegar, water, and artificial.

I try it. It's not horrible—until the aftertaste. I've chewed up enough pen tops to recognize plastic. I'm not sure if it's the cheese or the dressing, but I have definitely ingested something better suited for toys and writing utensils than human consumption. That's okay, though. I still have the entrée. And the pudding.

The microwave beeps. Finally, some real food. Lasagna is one of my all-time favorites. When I heard that it was one of the choices, I substituted it for the teriyaki-glazed pork chow mein, so I get to eat lasagna four times in the next two weeks.

I peel back the cover. That smell is back. What is it?

The lasagna still looks frozen, so I pop it back in for another minute. Still the same. Another minute. Then two. Finally, I realize that it's done, but the cheese doesn't melt. I compare the actual product to the picture on the box. They don't quite match. My dinner is about half the size, and the picture's cheese looks hot and melty. That's okay. It's the taste that matters, right?

I take a bite and chew slowly, exploring the texture, which is odd. Kind of grainy, kind of tomatoey, but mostly like a sponge. When I breathe through my nose, I taste that weird smell. I can't quite place it, but it reminds me of our garden. Kind of earthy. Like dirt. Oh my God, I'm eating dirt. It's probably all the whole grains and fiber. By the time I'm halfway through—three bites later, I swear—it almost tastes okay. Not Mom's lasagna, but edible.

I scrape every bit of sauce from the tray with my fork. Then I dig into the pudding. It has the same vitamin aftertaste as the Belly Buster, but it's still chocolatey and smooth. I devour it so fast that it doesn't matter. I'm still hungry, but after working out and eating everything I'm supposed to, I'm feeling pretty good about myself. I sip on a massive glass of water and think about how great I'll look on Jackie's wedding day.

I hide the package at the bottom of the garbage, rinse my dishes, and load them in the dishwasher so Mom doesn't ask what I ate. With the water running in the sink, I almost miss the phone ringing.

"Hello."

"Antoinette Galardi, please," says a voice. A man's voice. And so serious.

"This is Ann."

"This is Ron D—ski from the Twisted Pretzel." I don't catch his name, he says it so fast. "I'd like to have you in for an interview. When are you available?"

"Pretty much anytime."

"Is this evening too soon? I manage the stores in Lansing and Ann Arbor, too, so I'm only in Jackson a couple days a week."

"Sure." I run to the bathroom and look at my hair. Needs work before I can leave the house. "What time?"

"Five-thirty? Six?" he says. "I'm here until eight."

"I'll be there at six," I say, already plugging in the flat iron.

Wow! I just applied today. They must be desperate. That's good. Maybe I have a shot.

I throw myself together and leave a note for Mom. Now I have an excuse to be gone when they eat dinner. I just hope there aren't any leftovers because I'm already hungry again.

16

I WEAR THE SAME OUTFIT AS I DID FOR THIS MORN-
ing's interview. When I walk past Snapz! I see Ryann letting some
girls into dressing rooms. I could do that. But she didn't call me.
The guy from the Twisted Pretzel did.

When he shakes my hand, Mr. D—ski mumbles his name
again, so I still don't know what it is. He's kind of goofy and tries to
make jokes; I smile. He talks about Raynee and tells me that she
put in a good word for me.

"So what kind of experience do you have?" he asks.

I smell pretzels baking and my stomach gurgles. Loud. Like
there's a lion roaring in my gut. The picture on the wall of a giant
nacho cheese pretzel distracts me. I want one so bad, but my food
allotment for the day is up. It doesn't matter, though. Nothing
here is on the plan. I can't. I can't. I can't. Hey, didn't he just ask
me a question? What was it? Experience?

"I've never had an official job." I push the cuticle back on my
thumb and try not to fidget. "But I have lots of experience *buy-*

ing pretzels and *eating* them. And I have experience waiting on people. I have a needy family." I laugh nervously.

He laughs, too. "Well, we need someone right away. Raynee and Courtney are the only employees left. One girl is going away to college and the other one didn't work out. You wouldn't text your boyfriend while you're supposed to be working, would you?"

"No, sir. Of course not." I'm amazed that he thinks I could possibly have a boyfriend. I've never even been on a date.

"I know it's short notice, but can you start this week?" He fiddles with his watch. I'm sure he's checking the time, but he's pretty nonchalant about it. "Raynee will train you."

"I can start tomorrow, if you need me."

"Great," he says. "First, we need to get you a uniform shirt. We have a few in the back. What size do you wear?"

I panic. I do not like saying my size out loud. I don't even let salespeople find another size for me while I'm in the dressing room. I always get it myself.

Mr. D—ski opens a closet and pulls out a box with navy blue Twisted Pretzel polos in it. "Small? Medium? Large? Extra-large?"

I grab an extra-large. "This one will work."

"Good," he says. "The first one is complimentary. If you want any more, let me know, and I'll order them for you. Typically we wait until after the probationary training period of two weeks. I'll order your name tag today. *A-N-N*—no *E*, right?" I nod. "It should be in by the end of the week." He puts the box back into the closet and gives me a plastic Twisted Pretzel cup.

"This is for you. Unlimited refills. Just for you, though, okay?"

I nod. "If you leave it at home, you can use one paper cup per shift, but that's it. We keep track.

"Oh, and paydays are the first and fifteenth of the month. Corporate probably won't get all the paperwork until later in the week, so you won't get a check until the next pay period. Just so you know."

"Okay," I say. I quickly calculate the days until July 1. No pay for two and a half weeks? The S2S auto-shipment is in ten days! My heart pounds in my chest worse than when I was working out. The not-sufficient-funds panic swirls together with getting-a-job excitement.

When I get home, Mom, Mike, and the twins are eating dinner. Mom is coaxing Libby to eat. "It's good for you," she says. "It'll—"

"It'll put hair on your chest," says Mike.

"Daddy!" says Libby. "I don't want hair on my chest."

Mom gives Mike a fake-mad look and he smirks at her. Judd quietly eats his noodles. They look like the happy little family. I sneak upstairs to my room.

Later that night, I scan my Facebook newsfeed. Cassie posted pics of herself at Cedar Point amusement park with her friends. Cassie replied to one of the comments from Grace about the "pool party."

As I'm contemplating whether or not I should "like" it, Mom pokes her head in my room. "Hey, when did you get home?"

"A while ago." I look up from my laptop. "I got a job."

She's clearly surprised and pleased. "Great! Where?"

"The Twisted Pretzel. I start tomorrow."

"Really?" She scans my room. "What made you apply *there?*" Reading between the Mom lines, I take that to mean *The Twisted Pretzel is so fattening. I hope you don't actually eat there.*

"I applied at a bunch of places." I close the laptop. "They were the first to offer." And it's not really a lie.

"Good for you! Way to take some initiative! I'm glad to see you won't spend all summer watching TV." *Nope. I'm not totally lazy.*

"It's only part time and minimum wage—"

"You gotta start somewhere." She smiles.

"—but I'm pretty excited about it." I smile back.

"You should be! Congratulations!" She starts to leave but pauses. "And, Ann, do something about this room, will you?"

Minutes later I hear Mom's nightly ritual: the familiar clunk of the scales before the shower starts up. Next, she'll slather herself with lotion and wrinkle cream. Morning brings another weigh-in, washing and styling hair, and more moisturizing. Sometimes I wonder if Mom's beauty maintenance schedule is controlled by sunrise and sunset, or if it's the other way around.

17

ORDINARILY, PRETZEL-MAKING WOULDN'T SEEM like a big deal, but I'm a wreck on my first day of work. In fact, my stomach feels like a giant twisted pretzel.

Raynee's training me, so it isn't too bad. She shows me how to operate the cash register and where to hit it when the drawer sticks. She shows me where the supplies are and how to refill everything. I'm not sure what I thought was behind that small service area that the customer sees, but it's as unimpressive as the office at Snapz!. There's an oven, a freezer, a counter and sink, a storage closet, and a small bathroom. The whole place isn't much bigger than our laundry room.

Then we bake pretzels. I spray the baking sheets. "So is the nacho cheese still chunky?"

"No." She opens the box of frozen pre-fab pretzels. "I cleaned it out."

"What were the chunks?"

We plunk pretzels onto the sheets.

"I'm not sure, and I don't think I want to know."

I laugh.

Raynee puts the pretzels in the oven for ten minutes. Her glittery purple mascara matches her hair clips perfectly. Even her uniform shirt is perfect. Mine is like a box, droopy at the shoulders and tight around the middle. Hers hugs her waist and has little tucks and pleats in all the right places.

"Are the shirts you order different from the free ones?" I ask.

"No." Raynee grabs a spray bottle from a lower cabinet. "I alter mine."

"Yourself?" I'm surprised. Who does that?

Her cheeks flush. "Yeah. My whole family sews. It's no big deal."

Great. Now she probably thinks that I think she's weird or something. "That's cool," I try to cover. "I just didn't—"

"We're supposed to clean when there aren't any customers."

I drop it, but my gut doesn't, while I spray and wipe down the counter. I do think it's cool. Why do I always have to insert my foot every time I open my mouth?

A couple of kids come up to the counter. I watch Raynee help them. My stomach starts to settle down. This looks easy. So far, nothing I can't handle.

Then Jared Dunne—Raynee's boyfriend—stops at the counter. She tells him to buy something or leave. Correction: *ex-boyfriend*.

"I'm sorry, baby." He reaches for her, but she pulls away.

"Don't call me *baby*." She checks the straw holder, but we'd already filled it. I hate when guys call girls *baby*, too. It's so demeaning. "Better yet, never call me again."

After he storms off, Raynee tells me that he's cheated on her for the last time. She's not taking him back, she swears. She's done.

But the way she says it, I'm not sure if she's trying to convince me or herself.

Raynee looks like she's going to cry, so I tell her that I'll take the next customer.

"Okay," she says, and disappears into the back.

The next thing I know the cutest guy I've ever seen asks for a nacho cheese pretzel and a root beer. Nacho cheese, my favorite. *We were made for each other.*

He has short, sandy blond hair—natural, no weird hair products—and eyes the color of a chocolate Tootsie Roll pop. He's several inches taller than me but kind of stocky, wearing a bright blue polo shirt with a lanyard tag hanging around his neck. It's turned around, though, so I can't see his name or if he works at a mall store.

"Coming up." I smile and swipe his card. He smiles back. He has dimples! Oh, how adorable! Okay, this is way better than working at Snapz! Guys rarely come in there, unless they're with their girlfriends.

"Raynee or Courtney working today?" he asks when I hand him his root beer.

"Yeah," I take a waxed paper square and grab a pretzel from the warmer. "Raynee is. Want me to get her?"

"No, it's okay. I was just wondering."

At the nacho cheese reservoir, I look back and confirm, "Nacho cheese, right?" I knew. I just wanted to talk to him some more.

"You got it," he says, somewhat flirtatiously. Probably not, but that's how I imagine it.

I ladle the cheese and plan to carefully drizzle it over the pretzel in perfectly uniform swirls. That is not what happens. No swirls.

Not even streaks. And far from uniform. The whole thing drops in a puddle in the middle of the pretzel. It fills the holes and oozes underneath onto the waxed paper and down my wrist. When I turn around, the guy's eyes get wide, and his dimples are nowhere in sight. I know what he's thinking. He's wondering what's wrong with me. Any idiot can pour cheese on a pretzel, and here I am utterly pretzel challenged.

"I'm sorry." I watch the cheese drip onto the counter I just wiped down. "This is my first day, and this is actually the first pretzel I've ever made. I'll make you another one."

"Oh, no." He takes it from me. "It would be a shame to throw away your first effort. I'm honored to eat it."

I'm in love. Love with a capital *L*. This is the nicest guy I've ever met, not just the cutest.

"Really?" I cover my mouth, which has already decided to freeze into a smile without my consent. "You're not just saying that? Because I can make you another one. Or I can get Raynee. She actually knows what she's doing."

"No way." He looks at me and smiles. "I want to be your first."

Is he still talking about pretzels? My smile is gone. Dreamy guy turns creepy.

He must've realized what he said because all of sudden he blushes. "Oh!" he says. "Um, that sounded bad. Uh, I mean, uh, I meant your first *pretzel*." Cheese drips onto his arm.

Dreamy is back. He's adorable even when he's embarrassed.

I turn to grab a napkin, and in that split second, he leaves. I lean over the counter to see which way he went, but he's gone. Now I'll never get the chance to tell him everything is okay and that I'm not offended.

I decide that I will not touch a cheese ladle again until Raynee teaches me her technique. Especially for cute guys.

She's taking pretzels out of the oven when I go in the back. I tell her what happened, and we laugh, dubbing it the Nacho Fiasco.

The next few hours fly by! At one point, we have a rush, so Raynee and I have to move to keep up and not trip over each other. After a while, though, we get into a groove that's sort of fun—like I've worked there a long time. A few guys from the football team stop to see Raynee. She introduces me, but of course, I already know who *they* are.

While refreshing the pretzel warmer, she offers me one. "We're supposed to throw them away after a few hours, but sometimes Courtney and I eat them."

Yes, pretty please, with nacho cheese on top. I'm starving, and I can't eat my S2S lemon pepper chicken entrée until I get off at seven. "No thanks." I fill my plastic cup with Diet Coke. Then I fill Raynee's with Mountain Dew. We sit in the back and wait for the next batch to bake.

"Hey, what are you doing on the Fourth of July?" Raynee breaks off a piece of pretzel and pops it in her mouth.

The same as every year—nothing. "I don't know, why?"

She covers her mouth as she chews. Then she swallows and takes a drink. "We—Court, Mel, Tiff, and me—are having a party. It's an annual thing. Want to come?"

Raynee is asking *me* to a party? The Knees' Fourth of July party? It's always the talk of the first week of school. It's one invitation even Cassie never got. She always talked about going—more like showing up and hoping nobody noticed—but I never would. I want to text Cassie and tell her, but I know she'll crash it and say

I invited her. I feel guilty when I decide to wait and tell her about it *afterward*.

I think about how much weight I'll have lost by then—three weeks away. My biggest loss is always within the first two weeks. I could lose up to ten to fifteen pounds.

Maybe a Snapz! dress will fit—and not try to strangle me.

Or I might even be ready for a swimsuit.

I could start junior year thin *and* in on the jokes.

"Sure," I say. "Sounds good."

"Great! I'll give you more info when it gets closer." Raynee turns on the water in the sink and squirts in the soap.

I'm going to the Knees' party!

I never thought of cleaning as fun, but Raynee turns on music and dances and sings and blows suds at me. I laugh and wipe down counters, but I don't dance.

18

ELEVEN DAYS INTO MY S2S PLAN, I'M ANXIOUS TO weigh myself again. I lost seven and half pounds the first week, which is pretty typical for me. Usually that initial loss is big because I'm doing everything I'm supposed to do. Then I start slipping and gradually slide downhill from there—fewer and fewer pounds lost and hitting plateaus—until I fall off the wagon completely and start gaining again.

"Ready?" Mom stands in my doorway. She's been hounding me to go shopping all week, but I've been telling her I'm too busy. I am. Dodging dinner night after night. Hiding S2S packages. Working at the mall five days a week. Exercising whenever I'm home alone. Worrying that I won't get paid until four days after the next auto-shipment is scheduled.

"Yeah." I look up from my laptop. "Just give me a minute."

"Meet you in the car?" She mumbles something about not cleaning my room, but I ignore her, and she leaves.

Since the auto-ship is scheduled for tomorrow and I'm pretty much penniless for five more days, I need to cancel. I'll re-order once I get paid. I won't be able to afford a whole month, and it'll cost me more overall, but what choice do I have?

I go to the website, log into my account, and search for the checkbox the S2S operator mentioned. I can't find it. My profile only lets me change my password, email, and shipping address. Maybe it's under billing. Nope. Just options for paying, nothing for not paying. Maybe it's under food. Nope. Just plan choices and options for substitutions.

Mom beeps the horn. I slam my laptop lid. I'll have to deal with this later.

Before heading downstairs, I step on the scale. I'm only supposed to weigh once a week, but my shorts are feeling looser, so I just have to check. Why can't we have a digital scale where I can close my eyes as I get on and open them to see the ugly truth? No. We have to have a manual doctor's scale. I have to actually slide the indicator down the beam. To feel it move—either up or down—based on my actions. To be accountable.

Clunk. Clunk. Clunk. I set the indicator at my last weight. The weigh beam whacks up hard and bounces. I slide the marker over bit by bit until it balances. Two more pounds! That's nine and a half pounds in less than two weeks! I do a little shimmy and shake on the scale.

Eleven days of eating food that is barely edible. Eleven days of feeling hungry most of the time, yet still resisting giant pretzels and nacho cheese. Eleven days of forcing myself to work out, even if I can't follow Tia completely yet. Eleven days of hard work have paid off.

I'm ready to go dress shopping.

In the car on the way to the mall, I fantasize about the perfect dress—kind of short, kind of skimpy without being slutty, and totally figure flattering. It could even be a little tight to start. After all, I'm going to lose another thirty-five and a half pounds. Maybe I'll have to have it taken in at the last minute because it'll be way too big.

I'm so excited about losing almost ten whole pounds that I might even check out Snapz! after we're done in Keehn's formal department. Maybe there's a shirt or something that would fit now. One Snapz! shirt would push me to meet my goals. I know it would.

"Oh, Ann." Mom holds up a butter yellow chiffon knee-length dress. "What do you think of this one?" I wrinkle my nose. "Do they have a deep salmon? Or maybe iris?" Pinks, purples, and blues look best on me.

Too bad Mom would never go for black. Everyone looks good in black. And it's slimming. "This is a wedding, not a funeral," she says when I mention it.

Mom and I each grab several more dresses. We decide to each get what we like and then narrow the selection by what fits and what we agree on. Mom chooses from both the misses and juniors sections, sizes six and seven. Mine are all size seventeen, the biggest they have in juniors. Maybe one will be *too* big, and I'll have to say, "Mom, I'll be back. I need to get a smaller size."

The first dress—light pink, strapless—won't zip. Not at all. Must be sized wrong. I let it drop to the floor in a heap.

"Ooh, this one is so cute," Mom says from the next dressing room. "But it makes me look so pasty. I'll definitely need to get a spray tan before the wedding."

The next one—deep purple with a full, layered skirt, which I love!—is too tight to fit over my hips. I try putting it over my head but end up having Snapz! dressing room flashbacks and take it off, too.

"How are you doing, Ann?" calls Mom. "Find any keepers yet?"

The next one zips, but cuts off the circulation under my arms. It even leaves a mark. I could deal with being uncomfortable, but it forces my underarm fat up into a bulge. Great. A dress that makes me look even fatter!

"Oh my god, I am so fat!" exclaims Mom.

If you're fat, then I'm grotesque.

After three more dresses display my hideousness, I slide down the wall and onto the floor on top of the taffeta pile with my knees pulled to my chest. I've worked so hard for almost two weeks. Eating nothing that tastes good and still feeling hungry. Sweating. For nothing. I am still a blob. And the wedding is less than two months away. My throat tightens and my eyes burn. I give up. I freaking give up.

There's a knock on the door. "Ann?"

I ignore her. Tears puddle, and my nose tickles.

"Ann?" When I don't say anything, Mom bends down and peeks under the door. Her blonde ponytail falls in front of her upside-down face. "What are you doing?"

"Nothing. Leave me alone."

"We don't have to buy a dress here." Mom's voice is quiet, comforting. Tears stream down my cheeks. Uncontrollably. "Let me

101

in, honey. I'll help you get the dresses back on the hangers."

I don't say a word.

Next thing I know my picture-perfect-Barbie-doll mom is army crawling under the door of the dressing room. Raspy giggles escape around the lump in my throat. She inches over, carefully avoiding the dresses, and tries to put her arm around me. I pull closer to the corner, away from her, but she still tries.

"So these don't fit," she says. "We'll go somewhere else."

"It won't matter," I whisper into my knees. The tears start up again. Why does she have to be nice? Why can't she just wait outside and let me have a good cry? I don't want to talk about this. Especially not with her. She doesn't understand how I feel. Not even close. I don't want to hear her act all sympathetic like she gets it. I've seen her high school photos. She hasn't struggled with weight one day in her life.

"C'mon." She grabs my hands and pulls me to my feet. I hear someone else come into the dressing room area. If I don't move, Mom will keep talking, and I'll be even more embarrassed. I get up and start putting the dresses back on the hangers. Mom helps. I say nothing. Neither does she. But I see it. The pity. She feels sorry for me.

As soon as the car door closes, she starts in. "You know, if you want to lose weight, I can help."

Don't, Mom. Please. I look away and try to tune her out. Every word feels like a punch to the gut. I know she's trying to help, but it doesn't.

"All that fast food adds up. You've eaten at the mall most nights for the past two weeks. I've been meaning to talk to you about that, but I kept hoping it'd run its course."

You have no idea, Mom. No idea. Please stop. Please stop. Please stop.

"Lettuce on burgers does not count as a vegetable. From now on, I'll cook. We'll have steamed veggies and fresh fish or skinless chicken. We'll do it together. It wouldn't hurt any of us to eat healthier."

I sigh. Our house is only a few miles from the mall. I drive it every day. But it's never taken this long to get home. Why do we have to hit every red light?

"And it wouldn't hurt to get off the couch a bit, either. Sitting home all day—"

I can't take it anymore. "I get off the couch." I say. Quietly, but I say it.

"You'd be surprised how effective a simple walk can be," she continues. "All you have to do is—"

"I know what to do," I whisper. More for me than for her, I think. "I know what to do," I repeat, louder than a whisper but barely audible. "I know what to do." I don't hear her at all anymore. "I know what to do." Still to myself. "I know what to do."

She hears me and stops, both talking and driving. "What?" We sit at an intersection a few blocks from home.

"I know what to do." I still stare out the window.

"I know you've been on diets before, but—" The light turns green.

"I lied."

"What?"

"I lied," I say. "I haven't eaten at the mall for the past two weeks."

"What?"

"I've been on a diet. S2S. The Secrets 2 Success Weight Loss System. I bought it from an infomercial."

"An *infomercial?*"

"Yeah. It came with these awful supplements that I threw away because they made me jittery. Some of the food they sent is okay, but most of it is gross. I've been eating it anyway. And there's an exercise DVD, too. With resistance bands. I haven't been sitting on the couch all day. Well, I have some. But not all day. Not every day. I've been working out and working at the mall, too. And I haven't eaten there, either. Not once."

"Oh, Ann." She pulls in our driveway and turns off the car.

"I've been doing it for eleven days. I've lost almost ten pounds and used up most of my savings. But it's not enough. Still not enough."

Now Mom is speechless.

My reflection in the window stares at me. Stupid face. Stupid, ugly, fat face. All red and splotchy and fat. I open the car door and get out.

I head to my room. I have to cancel the auto-shipment. I don't have the money, and besides, it doesn't matter anyway. I'll probably always be fat. I might as well accept it.

I'll call Aunt Jackie and back out of being a bridesmaid, too. There's no way I'm wrapping myself in a bolt of shiny fabric and parading my fat ass down the aisle.

No way.

19

"HI, AUNT JACKIE," I SAY INTO THE PHONE WHILE opening my third S2S Belly Buster bar. I ate two getting up the nerve to make the call. It's not like it matters now. I take a big bite and chew.

"Hey, Ann. What's up?"

I swallow. "How are the wedding plans going?" I take another bite.

"Craptastic. I'm glad we're finally doing this, and I'm happier than I've ever been, but this wedding is a total pain in my ass. Just finding a place for the reception has been a nightmare. And the caterers! Chicken and fish or chicken and beef? We thought having a small wedding a couple months away would eliminate that year-long headache. Nope. It just adds more stress."

More stress? A bridesmaid dropping out might be kind of stressful, too.

I plop on the bed. My fat jiggles. "Mom and I went dress shopping today."

"Great! Did you find anything?"

"Nope." I sound pitiful. I wad up the wrapper and throw it on the floor. I open a fourth and take a bite.

"It's okay." Aunt Jackie picks up on my mood. "You'll find something. But you know, I don't care what you wear. Just as long as you guys are up there with us. Wear jeans and a T-shirt if you want."

I swallow hard, resolved not to disappoint Jackie. "I think I can wear something nicer than that. The day will be perfect. I just know it."

"I hope you're right," she says. "Hey, you're coming to the dance lessons, right?"

Oh, no. "What dance lessons?"

"Didn't your mom tell you? Chris signed up all us girls to learn all these dances—the Electric Slide, the Thriller, and a bunch of other crap. Mike would never do it, and you know Doug—he'd just make fun—so we skipped the guys. It'll be a hoot—you know, female bonding and all that."

"Mom hasn't mentioned it." Probably because Mom knows I don't dance in public.

"Six classes. Once a week. They start Tuesday night. Well, I gotta scoot. See you then."

I need to check the sticky note in my car to see if I'm scheduled to work Tuesday. Even if I'm not, I'll say I am.

So much for backing out. I'm starting to panic. I need more time. Time to lose weight. Time to find a suitable dress. Time before the auto-ship processes.

I log onto my S2S account again to cancel. Shouldn't it be on the page called auto-ship manager? It's not. I can give instructions on where to leave the food if I'm not home. Or I can upgrade to the super shipment that delivers two-month's worth for a fifty-cent per day savings. Why can't I find the DON'T-SEND-ME-ANY-MORE-I-FREAKING-GIVE-UP button?

I fish out the last Belly Buster bar in the box. May as well erase the evidence.

I click HELP. I search *cancel*. All I get is article results from their online magazine. I want to scream. I don't have money to buy the stupid food. But if I don't keep going, I'll be a cow at the wedding that I'm too chicken to back out on.

Chicken and beef. I hope Jackie goes with chicken and beef.

"Ugh!" I yell. Why does this have to be so complicated? No matter what I think about, I end up thinking about my next dinner. Why can't I just eat like a normal person?

After a quick knock on the door, Mom peeks in. "You okay?" Why can't I just eat like *her*?

"I don't know." I shove the empty wrappers in the box and nonchalantly hide them.

"There's a bridal/prom shop in Quincy." She opens the door and stands in the doorway. "Want to drive down there tomorrow?"

"No." I don't look up. I click over to Facebook.

"We have to keep trying," she says. Somehow I get the feeling she's not just talking about dresses.

"Uh-huh."

"I mean it."

She stands there, waiting, watching.

I stare at the dim Facebook notification bar. No response from Tony. I watch the ads blink next to it. Weight Watchers is offering a deal on membership. Even my computer is trying to tell me something.

She sits on the bed. She will not be ignored. "Tell me about this new diet plan."

"Nothing to tell. I'm done with it."

She stares at me, expecting more than that.

So I go back to the website and show her. She goes from page to page and reads about it. I pick up the Belly Buster box and look at the nutrition label. Each bar has two hundred calories! I ate the whole box in less than a half an hour. That's a thousand calories! Almost a full day's allotment. If I were going to purposely scarf down a thousand calories, I could have gone to Mondo Burger and made it worth my while.

"You said you used almost all of your savings?"

"Uh-huh."

"Is that why you want to quit?"

"Uh-huh." *That and the fact that I've worked so hard for two whole weeks and still see no difference.*

"Tell you what." Mom goes to a new page. "I'll transfer enough money into your account to cover the next shipment." She types in her banking info. "Then you buy the one after that. By then you should have enough. It's like we're splitting the cost. That'll cover you up to the wedding." She closes the laptop and puts her arm around me. "Deal?"

I shrink from her. Sure, she *is* bailing me out. And making it so I don't *have* to quit. But part of me wants to quit. This is hard. And I'll just end up failing again—I know it. The whole box of Belly Buster bars in my stomach is proof.

And now that she knows about it, I suddenly feel all this pressure to keep going. To do well. If it were still a secret and I failed, no one would know. But now? Now if I fail, I am even a bigger loser, especially compared to my mother, who never fails at anything. Now that she knows, she'll push. Push me to follow the plan to the letter. Push me to exercise. Push me places I'd rather not go. I hate pressure. Almost as much as I hate being a big loser. If only I were like the *Biggest Loser* instead.

But what choice do I have? Giving up now is instant failure. Just the thought of that feels like a brick in my stomach. Or maybe it's those bars. They're busting my belly, all right.

I suppose I can stick it out a little bit longer. At least there's hope in that. Slight as it may be.

"Deal," I say.

20

TUESDAY MORNING, MOM IS IN HER USUAL running-late frenzy. "Liberty!" she screams while she slathers peanut butter on bread. "Come on. Your cereal is getting soggy."

"I don't want it." Libby is glued to a cartoon on TV.

"You have to eat something." Mom slides the sandwiches into plastic bags. "We have to leave soon."

Libby ignores her.

"Don't you want to grow up big and strong?"

"Yeah," agrees Judd, milk dripping down his chin, his cereal half gone. "Like me and Ann."

Big and strong. Yup. That's me.

Judd's cereal has marshmallows and stars. Mine looks like the twigs that fall onto the lawn after a wind storm.

"No, thank you." Libby calls without taking her eyes from the TV. "I'm not hungry."

Mom sets the lunches by the garage door and stomps across the room. She flips off the TV and pulls Libby up. "It's breakfast time. Not TV time."

"I don't want it," she whines as Mom plops her into her chair. "The milk is ucky."

"It wasn't *ucky* a while ago. Eat it, Lib." I hate this. Mom used to make Tony eat, too. He was so stubborn—*strong-willed*, Gram says. That's probably why he's always been so skinny. Sometimes the battles would last for hours. Tony would sit and pout. Mom would yell. I would eat faster, hoping to make it all stop.

Libby takes a bite and spits it out. "Blech!"

Mom glances above the sink. Checking the time, no doubt. Weighing her options.

Even though she's lightened up a lot since Tony and I were little, my heart still races. Will she yell and rant? Or glare and slam? Hard to tell.

"Fine!" Mom picks up Libby's bowl and dumps it down the sink. "Let's go. I've got a lot to do today."

Judd puts his bowl in the sink and pushes in his chair. He knows the drill. *Mom is mad. Behave, or she'll turn on you, too.* I'm right there with him. I start unloading the dishwasher.

"I don't know why you pull this crap almost every morning." Mom grabs her travel coffee mug and her bag. Judd, grappling with their lunch and day care bag, heads through the garage door. Libby shuffles slowly behind him. By her set jaw, I can tell she's got an attitude. Man, she really does remind me of Tony.

After the car is loaded sans Libby, Mom returns and grabs her arm. Libby pulls back, but Mom is stronger. She practically drags her to the car. "I'm hungry," I hear Libby whine as the garage door slams.

The car starts but doesn't leave right away. Within a minute, Mom returns. She opens the cupboard door and rips open a box of

Pop-Tarts. I can't believe she's giving Libby a Pop-Tart. There is no way—I mean *no way*—she would have ever let me or Tony pull that.

"What do you want me to do?" Mom reads my glare correctly. "Donna freaks out if the kids haven't eaten breakfast when I drop them off. I don't have time to fight today."

Mom must be getting old. Not only did she always have time for a fight, I used to think she *made* time for them. I've got to hand it to Libby, though. She's showing Mom a thing or two about food manipulation.

"Oh, by the way," says Mom, halfway out the door. "You get out of work at four today, right?" I nod. "Good. We have dance lessons tonight. All of us—you, me, Gram, Jackie, Tayla, Chris, and some of Chris's family." Before I could protest, she adds, "*All* of us. It's nonnegotiable," and slams the door.

Damn it. I planned to tell her my schedule was changed, but she caught me off guard. How can dance lessons be nonnegotiable? I decide right then that I'll pull a Libby. She can make me go, but she can't make me dance.

~~~~~

I have a short shift at work today—noon to four—and I work with Courtney. When I get there, she's in the back on her cell. "No way! Stop! . . . No, *you* stop!" I say hi, and she nods dismissively. Talking to her boyfriend, no doubt. Her obnoxious, flirty voice gives her away.

There's a line of customers and the pretzel warmer is empty.

"Just a second," I say to an annoyed guy at the counter and rush to check the oven. It's empty. Nothing on the counter either. "Pretzels?" I ask Courtney.

She shrugs as if to say, *What do you want me to do about it?* and points to the freezer, not even taking the phone from her ear.

You've got to be kidding me! Has she done anything today?

I slam the baking sheets onto the counter, fill them, and pop them in the oven. At least it's already on and warm! Then I go back to the counter and say, "I'm sorry. It'll be about ten minutes."

"Are you serious?" the man yells. "I've already been *waiting here* ten minutes! What have you been doing back there, eating them all?" A kid in line behind him laughs.

"I'm sorry, sir," I try to explain, fighting the lump forming in my throat. "I just got—"

"—hungry, I know." The guy cuts me off and now several people laugh. "Forget it." He looks at my name tag. "Ann. Your manager will be hearing about this." He storms off before I can apologize again.

"I'll be right back." I say and run to the bathroom. I shove my name tag in my pocket and take a few deep breaths to keep from losing it. Then I dab my face with wet paper towels. When I come out, the timer is going off and Courtney is MIA. I want to scream! Aren't we supposed to be working together? I fling open the oven and grab the tray—with my bare hand—and then drop it. *Crash!* Pretzels all over the floor.

I scream. "Aaargh!" My hand hurts like hell, and I want to get out of here.

I'm running cool water over my hand when Courtney finally shows up. "What are you doing? There's an angry mob forming out here!" Then she sees the pretzels all over the floor and cracks up, laughing. Like a freaking bleach blonde hyena.

I manage to get another tray of pretzels in the oven, despite my throbbing hand, and Courtney gives everyone in line free drinks *for being so awesome*. After the timer buzzes, I grab the tray—using an oven glove this time—and take them to the front. By now, the angry mob has dwindled to two kids waiting for plain pretzels, no salt. I hand them over the counter, and they run to their mother.

Courtney is sitting on the step stool, drinking pop (from a paper cup and in front of customers—both no-no's), and talking to a couple of guys. And one of them is that guy from my first day—the cute one with the dimples! I load the warmer and try not to stare. "Last year's party is nothing compared to what we have planned this year." Courtney sees me but doesn't acknowledge me. "*Everybody* is going to be there."

"Hey, Pretzel Girl," Dimple Guy says. *Is he talking to me?*

I look up and he smiles. *Oh God, I'm melting.* Seriously. I'm a sweaty mess. Wet paper towels, a hot kitchen, and frustration overload will do that.

"Hey," I say.

"How do you know my cousin?" Courtney asks, which sounds like an accusation.

Cousin? Dimple Guy is related to Courtney? You've got to be kidding me!

"He was my first—" I pause trying to think of something witty.

"Your first what?" she sneers.

Dimple Guy laughs at Courtney's reaction, which makes me

and the other guy laugh, too. Chalk one up to unintentional wit. "Wouldn't *you* like to know?" he says playfully.

She glares at him, and he smirks. *Ooh! He's an instigator, like Tony.* Except this time the button-pushing is all in fun. He doesn't say another word. He simply winks at me and leaves.

"Hey," calls the other guy as he runs to catch up. "Wait up!"

"Ugh! He's so annoying!" Courtney pulls a pretzel out of the warmer and bites into it.

I spray down the counter and wipe it and pretend I didn't hear her. He's not annoying at all. He's adorable.

"He'd better not come to my party." *Oh, so it's* her *party now?* She takes another bite before tossing the pretzel into the garbage. What a waste!

"Is he invited?" I ask, trying not to sound too eager.

"Duh! Of course."

I wonder if Raynee's told her that I'm invited, too. Probably not.

Courtney and I avoid each other the rest of the shift. I want to ask her more about her cousin, and she's obviously curious about how I know him. But pretending that he and I have something to tell makes it feel almost real. If I start talking, I'll have to admit that I don't even know his name.

21

THE BURN ON MY HAND DOESN'T HURT MUCH BY
the time I get home, but I wrap it in gauze and tell Mom it does. "I
can't dance," I say.

"Let me see," she says. I take off the bandage. "Get in the car."

Michael Jackson's "Thriller" blasts from the dance studio in
Spring Arbor as we walk in. The video plays on a monitor in the
corner. My stomach flutters. Just the thought of dancing—more
like jiggling and tripping—in front of people makes me want to
puke up my S2S turkey and roasted red pepper panini with baked
sweet potato fries. I stretch out the bottom of my T-shirt to make
it look roomier and readjust my shorts. I hate how they always ride
up when I walk. Nothing draws attention to thunder thighs more
than shorts riding up your crotch.

Gram shows up wearing yellow and white striped knee socks
and ancient white Reeboks. Her hair is in high pigtails, and her
hot pink terry cloth headband matches her stretchy shorts. Her
Mackinaw City T-shirt has pink and yellow and green seagulls on
it. She's coordinated and ready to jam. I know this because she

walks into the room and exclaims, "We're jamming now!" I'm not even sure what that means, but the perky blonde dance instructor, Laura, seems amused.

Mom's outfit matches, too—navy bike shorts and a pink tank with navy piping—but she looks like *she* could be the dance instructor.

We bring the twins because Mike has to work late. They run around in circles on the dance floor.

Aunt Jackie, Chris, and her sisters, Carrie and Lisa, arrive together, along with Uncle Doug's girlfriend, Tayla, who is not Mom's and Aunt Jackie's favorite person. Mainly because she and Uncle Doug fight, break up, and get back together constantly, and Tayla posts every detail on Facebook. I like her well enough, but Mom says that's because she's closer to my age than Doug's.

Gram throws her arm around my shoulders and pulls me in. "Don't we look like the cat's pajamas," she says to our images in the floor-to-ceiling, wall-to-wall mirror.

"Yeah, Gram," I say. "Cat pajamas. Just the look I was going for."

She kisses my head and then starts stretching out like she's about to run a marathon.

"Okay, let's get started," says Laura, with a smile. "Everyone up. Space yourselves in two rows. Use the dots on the floor to help you."

Mom steps onto the dot in the back. "Wait. We have one more person coming."

"We do?" asks Jackie. "Who?"

"Regina," says Mom, fighting back a smile.

"You are not serious! Are you?"

Mom cracks up.

Chris, her sisters, Gram, and I laugh, too.

So does Aunt Jackie. "Shut up. I hate you." She stands on the dot in front of Mom and gives her a little shove. I wonder if Libby and I will tease each other someday.

Jackie, Tayla, Chris, Carrie, and Lisa are in front—the row closest to the wall-size mirror. I stand along the back wall, trying to blend into the barre. "There's plenty of room over there." Laura points to the corner next to Gram as she has Libby and Judd stand next to Mom.

"That's okay. I'm fine right here."

Mom glares and gives me her move-it-now head jerk. I take my time getting there, wishing I'd be let off the hook like Mike, Uncle Doug, and Chris's brother-in-law. Nobody even asked them, let alone forced them.

We're lined up and ready to go. I catch a glimpse of myself in the mirror and move so that Chris is directly in front of me, blocking my view.

"Okay," says Laura. "Let's begin with some basic steps without the music. Step, touch right. Step, touch left." We follow, looking deader than the zombies from the video. "Good. It's okay to smile. This is supposed to be fun. Now let's add the arms. Sweep across as you step."

We sweep. It's slow enough that I don't jiggle. I'm grateful.

Within minutes, the music is on and we're stepping and turning and stepping and turning again. I can't keep up. I step with the wrong foot and turn the wrong way. Mom, Jackie, Carrie, and Lisa, who are all athletic, have the footwork, arms, and attitude down by the second time through. Gram, of course, doesn't follow directions. She just does her own thing, which includes an extra helping of Thriller claws. She adds a roar with each one, usually at Tayla, who, like Chris, isn't as graceful as the others, but they're both holding their own. Even the twins are stepping, turning, and clawing their way across the floor. Maybe not in synch with the music, but they are so stinking adorable it doesn't matter.

Even though I've been doing my S2S exercise DVD every day for the past two weeks, I'm still out of breath. Few things are more embarrassing than being shown up on the dance floor by your four-year-old twin siblings and your sixty-year-old, chain-smoking grandmother. Good thing Gigi's not here, because even she dances better than I do. I scan the room and realize that I am the fattest person in it. The fattest, even though I'm almost the youngest.

The fattest.

The slowest.

The most likely to be picked off first by the Thriller zombies.

I can't take it anymore. As soon as Laura starts the song again, I slip out of the room, sit on a bench, and watch through the window.

I watch through "Thriller" and the Electric Slide and some other line dance I've never heard of. Everyone steps and stomps and sweats for nearly two hours. But most of all, they laugh. They're all having a great time. Chris missteps but doesn't seem to care. Tayla's butt jiggles, but she just shakes more. Everyone laughs.

Everyone but me.

22

AFTER DANCE CLASS, EVERYONE IS SO PUMPED
that they decide to go for ice cream.

"We have to pass," says Mom.

She winks at me, like she's doing it for me. But going for ice cream is something that I actually *want* to do. Unlike dancing in front of people. I could get a mini cone. It wouldn't be that bad.

"Aw, come on, Suzy!" Jackie fake-whines like a little kid.

Chris and her sisters wait in their car, and Gram and Tayla wait for the verdict. Both of them suck on cigarettes like they're coming up for air after two hours under water.

Mom shakes her head and pops the twins into the van. "The twins need to get to bed."

"No we don't, Mommy!" protests Judd.

"I want ice cream," says Libby.

Mom sticks to her guns. "Sorry."

"What about Ann?" Gram jingles her keys. "Can't she go? I can bring her home later."

I love you, Gram.

"Ann has to work in the morning. She's opening. Aren't you, Ann?" Mom says pointedly.

"It's really not that late," I say. "And we don't open until ten."

"Ann? We're going dress shopping again this weekend. Are you sure you want ice cream?"

Gram glares at Mom. "God, Suzy! What are you doing?"

"You don't understand, Ma." Mom's voice raises about an octave. "Ann *wants* to lose weight for the wedding. I'm not making her. She even bought a diet off TV, for crying out loud. Used her savings to do it. So don't look at me like I'm the bad guy."

Oh God! Kill me now.

Gram turns to me. "You *bought* that?" She seems shocked.

"You knew?" Now Mom is shocked.

Laura comes out and locks the studio. "Is everything okay?"

I smile. *Everything's fine. We're just arguing about whether or not the fat girl needs ice cream.*

"Just talking," says Gram. "See you next week."

Laura waves and clicks the remote for her car. Tayla goes over to talk to Chris and Jackie. I'm sure she's giving them a play-by-play.

After an awkward silence, Mom slams the van door and walks to the driver's side. "We're going home."

After Gram hugs me and kisses my cheek, she walks away shaking her head.

As soon as we're in the car, Mom explodes. "I don't get it." She slaps the steering wheel. "One minute I think you want to lose weight. You want to fit into a nice dress for the wedding. I try to help you. I pay for that food. I buy lots of salad stuff. When Jackie suggested these classes, I thought you'd be all over them. It's exercise and it's fun and we'll learn some moves for the wedding. But you sulk outside and want to go for ice cream!" She puts the car in drive. "Explain it to me, will you?"

I don't know what to say. She's right. It doesn't make sense. I *do* want to lose weight. Except I just want it to . . . happen—without all the work and deprivation.

Not eating ice cream and real food sucks. But being afraid to let loose in front of people sucks, too. I miss out on so much—like dancing and bike riding and wearing bikinis and cute clothes—because I'm fat. And then I miss out on ice cream and family dinners and giant pretzels with friends because I'm trying *not* to be.

And that's the reason I didn't want anyone to know about the new diet.

The routine is always the same. First, there's pity: *The poor little fat girl needs help because she's too stupid to know what to eat and how much.* Then, there's pressure: *No, no, no, you don't need that. That's enough of that.* Then, there's disappointment: *What's the matter with you? Why can't you just follow the plan?* Followed lastly by disgust: *We just ate four hours ago. I'm still so full. How can you be hungry?*

And it's starting all over again.

"Well, are you going to answer me?" Mom alternates between watching the road and trying to make eye contact.

Only I won't let her. I stare out the side window. I can't face her. She doesn't understand. She's never been fat. She's never struggled with self-control. She's never been *out* of control. Not a day in her life. I can't talk to her about this.

Slimmer You says, "Picture yourself thin to ward away cravings." I close my eyes and picture it. Then I picture ice cream. I still want it. And I hate myself for it.

23

THE NEXT AFTERNOON I WORK WITH BOTH RAYNEE
and Courtney. When I get there, I overhear Courtney say something like, "I can't believe you invited her."

"I like her, okay?" Raynee says.

Are they talking about me? I try to blend into the door frame,
but it's too late. They see me.

"Whatever." Courtney bites into a pretzel fresh off the tray and
pours nacho cheese into a cup. "Oh my God, I'm starving." Then
she changes the subject to Raynee's boyfriend.

"It's over," says Raynee. "And I mean it this time."

"Geez, Rayne, he said he was sorry." She dips her pretzel in the
cheese. "How are we going to double-date if you don't take him
back?"

"We'll see . . ." She doesn't seem convinced.

From what I can see, this guy makes her miserable, not happy.
Is a relationship even worth the eventual heartache of a break-
up? For example, nobody can imagine Uncle Doug and Tayla living
happily ever after. So why do they keep trying? If I were Raynee,

I'd cut my losses and move on, like both of my parents did. But how would I know? I've never met anyone worth the risk. Not yet, anyway.

After Courtney devours her third pretzel, I pull out a pan to bake more. Where does she put it all? She eats more pretzels than I ever have, and she's practically half my size.

After the pretzels are in the oven, I fill my plastic Twisted Pretzel cup with Diet Coke.

"Hey, Ann," Courtney calls. "Get me an orange pop, will you?"

"Where's your cup?"

"I forgot it at home. Just grab a paper one." Another rule broken.

She and Raynee are party planning. I bet they discuss decorations more than Jackie and Chris discuss caterers for their wedding. Streamers and balloons? Or red and white sparkly lights with blue tablecloths?

I hand Courtney her pop and jump in the conversation. "You know you can order custom M&M's online? You could get red, white, and blue ones with your own messages on them."

"M&M's?" Courtney wrinkles her nose.

"I'll check them out," says Raynee, but she probably won't. Maybe Raynee doesn't really want me to come either.

I head out front to open the cash register. Giggling bursts out behind me. Courtney said something about me, I know it. I like working alone with Raynee better.

A while later as I'm refilling the straw dispenser, a familiar voice says, "Ann! When did you start working here?"

It's Dad. And Nancy. And Nate, Naomi, and Noah. The perfect family out and about. A family that I'm supposed to be part of—but I'm not.

"A couple weeks ago." I'm not sure what else to say. I haven't talked to or seen Dad in months.

We stopped talking after Godzilla booted Tony, and Dad hasn't called. It's not like he went out of his way for me much, anyway. I used to dream about him ditching one of Nate's or Naomi's meets or a church service to hang out with me and Tony. Or better yet, inviting us to go with him and really meaning it. Including us for real. I used to dream that the Polar Express was real, too.

"Hi, Ann!" Nancy says in her fake-nice voice. She has a new trendy haircut. "Have you lost weight?"

Wow! I'm taken aback. Nancy noticed. She's the first. I'm not sure if I should be flattered or offended. Whenever I lose weight and this happens, it always makes me cringe. It reminds me that people *do* notice, which makes me even more self-conscious.

"A little," I say.

"Great! Keep it up," she says. What's that supposed to mean? I'm sure she thinks she's being supportive, but I hear, *What a huge job you have ahead of you! Better you than me.*

"Thanks."

"Could I get a plain pretzel, no salt, with mustard and a small lemonade for Naomi?" she asks.

I grab a cup and scoop ice into it. "Yeah, no problem."

Noah squirms in his stroller. I can't believe how big he is. The last time I saw him, he was tiny. Nate sits at the tables in the middle of the mall, looking bored out of his mind, and Naomi looks up from her cell to nod at me.

Courtney rushes out from the back and fake-hugs her. "Hey, girl! I haven't seen you all summer. You'll be at the big Fourth of July bash, right?"

I push the cup into the dispenser.

"Wouldn't miss it," says Naomi. Then her phone vibrates. She checks it, laughs, and replies. When she's done, I hand her the cup and the pretzel. Dad pulls out his debit card. "That'll be—" I say, but Courtney interrupts me.

"Oh, don't worry about it. Naomi's my friend. It's a perk to working here."

It is? That's not what Mr. D—what's-his-name told me when I got hired. And I've never seen Raynee do it. I don't say anything, though. Courtney's worked here way longer than I have. Maybe it's an unsaid kind of perk.

"Mom," says Naomi. "Amber's waiting for me at Vicky's. Then we're going to Snapz! Once I find a swimsuit, I'll text you."

Vicky's? Are Naomi and Victoria so close that they're on a nickname basis? She probably even knows her secret. Victoria doesn't share her secrets with fat chicks.

"So you didn't find one at Keehn's that day?" I ask.

"Yeah." Naomi laughs. "But you just can't have too many swimsuits, can you?"

I'd be happy with one.

"Okay," says Godzilla. "Remember, modest is hottest."

Naomi rolls her eyes, waves to Courtney and me, and walks away. Once she's gone, Courtney disappears into the back. Nate takes off shortly after without a word—to find a cooler crowd, no doubt.

There is a weird awkward silence. Until Noah screeches and bows his back. Dad unbuckles him and picks him up.

"Hey," says Nancy. "What are you doing tonight?"

"Me?" I ask.

"Yes, you." She laughs like I said something ridiculous. Like she asks my schedule every week.

"I don't know. Why?"

Nancy looks at Dad, and he smiles and nods. "Well, we have this Family First thing at church . . ."

Family First? For real? Does that include the first family, too, or just the new one?

Noah leans forward, propelling himself from Dad to Nancy, and screeches again. She takes him and bounces him on her hip. "I'm sure Noah would love to see you, wouldn't you, buddy?" He grins a wide toothy baby grin.

"Yeah." Dad seems genuinely excited. "I'll even treat for Napanelli's."

Napanelli's has a deep-dish pizza that is to die for. Not quite on the S2S plan, but if I don't eat anything for the rest of the day, I'm sure one slice won't hurt me. Besides, time with Dad—even if Nancy and her kids are there, too—sounds great. Maybe it's the first step to having a real relationship. Something I haven't let myself think about for a long time.

"Okay." I smile. A Wednesday night thing at their church—about putting family first. And they want me to go with them. Really want me to go.

"How about I pick you up around six-thirty?" asks Dad.

"I can drive now," I say.

"Better yet. See you later, sweetie." They head down the mall,

Dad pushing the stroller, Nancy wrestling with Noah. By the time they get to the cell phone kiosk, Dad's carrying Noah, and Nancy's got the stroller.

Sweetie. The last time Dad called me that he could lift me over his head and I was missing half of my front teeth.

A family thing. Tonight. With Dad. I can't wait.

24

I PULL UP TO DAD'S FIFTEEN MINUTES EARLY. I don't want them to have to wait for me. One more quick check in the rearview mirror. Am I dressed okay? I don't know what kind of family thing this is. A festival? A dinner? A service? Can't be dinner because Dad's ordering Napanelli's first. I went for a casual dressy look—a flowy cotton skirt, a polo, and my nicest flip-flops. That should cover whatever it is.

The garage is open. Should I go through there—the way the family does—or around to the front door, like company? I opt for family. My flip-flops slap on the concrete garage floor. Nate and Naomi come out before I have a chance to knock.

"Hey," I say to them.

"Hey," they mumble. Nate fumbles for his keys, and Naomi heads for the passenger side of Nate's sporty little red compact. Did Dad pay for that?

"Aren't you going to that family thing tonight?" I ask them.

Naomi laughs. I guess that's her answer.

Okay. Whatever. I'm not going to complain about getting Dad mostly to myself.

I knock on the open kitchen door and walk in. "Hey, Dad? Nancy?"

"Hey, sweetie." Dad kisses my cheek. "I'm so glad you were free tonight. This means a lot to me."

"Me too, Dad." And I mean it.

"How about I order the pizza? Do you still like pepperoni, ham, and mushroom?"

"Sure do," I say.

He picks up the phone and dials. "A medium should be big enough, don't you think?"

Ordinarily I can eat a medium by myself. But since I plan to have only one slice and Dad and Nancy probably won't pig out, I'm sure it's fine. I nod. *Slimmer You* says to fill up on good stuff like raw veggies or salad greens before starting on heavy foods like pizza, to keep from overeating. The S2S booklet encourages salad with most every meal.

"Could you get a salad, too?" I ask Dad while he's on hold. "Tossed with light Italian dressing?"

"No problem."

I sit on the couch and wait. The living room is the same as it's always been, except now there are a lot more toys around. They have an updated family pic above the piano. They're all wearing red. I imagine where Tony and I would fit if we'd been there. We'd stand behind Dad. Nate and Naomi would stand behind Nancy, and Noah could still sit on her lap. It would be balanced, and look just as nice as it does now. They each have a teenaged boy and girl.

It could have worked out, I tell myself. It could have. But it hasn't.

Dad recites his credit card number into the phone. He winks at me.

Maybe it still could work out. Maybe their next family pic *could* include Tony and me. Or if Tony is still bitter, at least me. I could stand at Dad's left shoulder. And since I'd be thinner by then, I would stand tall and smile, just like Naomi.

"Okay." Dad hangs up. "Pizza should be here in about forty-five minutes."

"What time does the family thing start?"

"Seven."

Seven? That's in fifteen minutes. How will we have time for dinner?

Nancy bursts into the room with Noah on her hip. She sets him down on his feet, and he's off. He not only walks, but runs. Everywhere.

"Oh my gosh!" she says. "It's six forty-five already? We need to get moving." She starts talking in hyper-speed, grabbing stuff, and pointing. "Noah's jammies are set out on the changing table. He'll eat pizza if the pieces are cut small enough. Just a few at a time, or he'll toss them on the floor."

What? Why is she telling me this? Isn't Noah coming with us?

"There's a nighttime bottle in the fridge. Don't let him see it before eight thirty, or he'll cry until he gets it. . . ."

Dad hands Nancy her purse. "Everything will be fine. I'm sure Ann has everything under control. It's not like this is her first time babysitting."

Nancy continues babbling on about the bottle and warming it, but I don't hear her. *Babysitting?*

They asked me over to babysit?

To babysit.

Baby. Sit.

To be the babysitter.

Not the daughter.

Not part of the family thing at church.

But the babysitter.

"Is something wrong?" asks Nancy. I can't imagine what my face looks like. Confused? Stunned? Incredulous? Blindsided? Hurt? I hadn't thought about hiding my reaction. I hadn't thought. *Pull it together. Suck it up.*

"No," I lie. "Everything's fine. Have fun." My voice squeaks. Probably because every muscle in my body is clenched tight.

"Okay," says Dad. "See you around ten."

As soon as the door closes, Noah freaks out. Not just crying—screaming at the top of his lungs. He slams himself against the door and beats his head on it. I'm worried that he's going to give himself a concussion. Of course they'll blame the babysitter. The babysitter. A daughter would never hurt her baby brother. But a babysitter? A babysitter is essentially a stranger. And that's how Noah sees me, too. I can't exactly blame him.

I pick him up, and he arches his back and kicks. Then he goes limp, trying to slide out of my arms. When the twins do that, Mike calls it "the wet noodle." Kids are impossible to hold onto when they do that, and they know it. Noah is a master. I try distracting him. With toys. With TV. With looking out the window at birds and cars. Nothing works. He screams and cries. "Mama . . . No . . . Mama . . ."

"She'll be back soon," I coo as soothingly as I can.

I know how he feels. Duped. I feel the same way. He probably thought he'd be hanging with his mom and dad tonight, too. *Family First*, my ass.

After what seems like hours of Noah's crying, the pizza guy shows up. Noah pauses his screaming long enough to ask, "Who is it?" when the guy comes to the door. Long enough for me to open the door and grab the pizza and salad.

When I try to put him in his high chair, he screams again. I back off and put him down. He runs around while I sit at the table alone and dig into the salad. I chew and chew and think about all the strategies I had planned: I was going to eat slowly, chew thoroughly, and sip water between bites. I was supposed to share a medium with the family, so I couldn't overeat. I stare at the pizza—whole and untouched—and toss the salad into the garbage.

Once I start eating my pizza, Noah wants a bite. I break off a piece and give it to him. Then I cut some of it into little pieces. He comes back for more. Like a dog. I always hated when the twins did that, but I'm desperate to make the kid happy. It seems to be working.

Until . . .

Until I open the fridge. Just long enough to grab a Diet Coke. That's all it takes. Noah sees his bottle and starts screaming again. It's not 8:30 yet but close enough for me. I try to remember what Nancy said about warming it. Do it? Not do it? In the microwave? Not in the microwave? I don't know. I almost don't care. I hand it to him, and for the first time since I got there, he's quiet.

While he's occupied, I change his diaper and put him in his pajamas. Within a half an hour, he's drained his bottle and crashed on the floor. He really is kind of cute when he's not busting open my eardrum. I scoop him up and lay him in his crib.

Then the real challenge begins. When Noah was screaming and running around, I was busy. Too busy to think about anything. Now as I sit on the couch and stare at the TV, my stomach churns along with my head.

I review the day and try to figure out how I could have misunderstood Dad and Nancy. I can't figure it out. Do I want a normal relationship with my dad so badly that I hallucinated? Did they trick me? Is Nancy an evil Godzilla, like Tony thought? I don't know, but what I do know is that the pizza is the best thing I've eaten in weeks. One more slice couldn't hurt, could it?

I try to think of Jackie's wedding and how I want to look. I try to be strong. Mom is right. It doesn't make any sense to want one thing and do the opposite. But somehow there's a disconnect between my brain and my stomach. Somehow my stomach got connected to my heart.

Over the next hour and a half I wage war on that pizza's temptation. I cut the slices in half, thinking just a little more will satisfy me. And a little more. Two and a half slices later, it dawns on me. Pizza is not what I'm hungry for. But it's better than making a scene with Dad and alienating him completely. Better than creating more awkward silence.

Tonight, pizza is the best I can do.

25

WHEN I GET HOME, MOM IS STILL AWAKE, READ-
ing in bed. As I pass by, she asks, "Well, how did it go?"

"Fine." I don't want to talk about it. I just want to go to my room.

"Fine?" She sits up. "What's wrong?"

I stop in her doorway but talk quietly because Mike is asleep. "They didn't want me to go with them. They wanted me to *babysit*."

"Oh, honey! I'm sorry," Mom says a bit louder. Mike stirs but doesn't wake up.

"It's fine." I lie.

"Did he pay you, at least?"

"No." I don't tell her that he tried. That I wouldn't take it. That I said, *We're family, Dad.* And that he kissed my forehead and let me leave, like everything was normal.

I'm done. I refuse to make any more excuses for him. He doesn't even know me. He can't read me like Mom. I want to go in and curl up next to her, like I used to. "I'm going to bed." I say.

"Good night." Then I'm pretty sure that under her breath she mutters, "Dickhead."

"What?" Mike asks groggily.

"Nothing," she says. "Ann's home. Go back to sleep."

~~~

I'm so drained that I melt into my pillow. Just as I start to doze, I visualize myself running. My perfect, athletic body—hey, it's my imagination, may as well make it good—striding rhythmically and harmoniously in time to the music playing in my ears. I run for miles and miles. I do not sweat, only glisten, and my face is not red. My shoes are worn and hug my feet from all the miles we've traveled together.

I run from my troubles. From Mom and her pressure. From Dad and his distance. From Tony and his absence. From Mike and the twins and their presence. I run the fat and the sadness away. There is no jiggle.

In my dream, running feels like flying. Smooth. Freeing. Although I've never run before—or played any sports, really—I imagine that is what's it's like.

I'll get some new running shoes. As soon as I get paid. Monday. Monday. A new week. A new month. A new start.

Monday I will start running.

july

26

MONDAY MORNING, I FINALLY GET THE COURAGE
to weigh myself again. I avoided my last scheduled weigh-in
because of the box of Belly Buster bars and the Napanelli's pizza. I
wanted to get a few successful days under my belt first. Which I've
done. Just like *Slimmer You* says: "When you slip up, don't despair.
Get back on track right away." Typically, for me, a slip-up is the
beginning of the end. Not this time, though. I'm pretty proud of
myself. But I'm still afraid.

I take a deep breath and step onto the scale.

Clunk, clunk.

My stomach flutters. I have exercised. I've eaten according to
plan, most of the time. But is that enough? I slide to where I was
the last time, nine days ago. *Clunk!* I inch it a bit more—a half
pound, then another, and another. It balances.

I've lost another pound and a half. I should be excited. I've lost
eleven pounds! At least I didn't *gain*. But a measly pound and a half
after sweating with Tia and starving doesn't seem like much. I was
hoping for at least two or three more. *Slimmer You* says, "Don't be

discouraged by the scales. Exercise builds muscle, which weighs more than fat. Eating right and exercise pays off over time. Keep it up."

Yeah, okay, *Slimmer You*. But I still have thirty-four more to go. And time is ticking. The wedding is only six and half weeks away.

The house is quiet. Mom, Mike, and the twins have already left. I decide to skip breakfast despite S2S and *Slimmer You* both touting it as "the most important meal of the day." I don't care. I need faster results.

My first paycheck should be ready today. I plan to save most of it for the next S2S shipment, but I want to buy a pair of running shoes, too. Then I can really speed up the process. Do you have any idea how many calories running burns? Lots. Whoever heard of a fat runner? No one. Running practically ensures fitness. Mom swears by it. She runs two or three miles a day, even in crappy weather.

I pull my hair back and head for the mall. Courtney and Raynee are working. They're talking about the party when I get there—it's three days away!

"Aren't you excited?" Raynee asks me.

Courtney doesn't say anything. I know she doesn't want me to come. Maybe Courtney will like me more if I bail and stay home. That doesn't make sense, but I still feel it. Maybe it'll make me look less desperate to be popular. Less desperate always equals more cool. But I am more desperate, less cool.

I leave them to their private planning and giggling and deposit my check at the bank across the street from the mall.

The sporting goods store, with all the treadmills, ellipticals, balls, and gear, feels like a locker room. Some place I do not belong.

The girl at the register looks at me but says nothing. I know she's thinking: *What are* you *doing here?*

I go to the back and scan the wall of shoes. They all look the same.

A voice startles me. "Can I help you?"

It's the guy! Dimple Guy! Courtney's cousin!

"Hey. I didn't know you worked here," I say, like a lame-o freak. Like we're friends. Like I know all about him and his life. And his name.

"Yeah, I work here. For this stylin' outfit, which is way better than my weekend apron."

I must look confused because he clarifies. "I work for my aunt's catering business on weekends. What can I do you for, Ann? Or should I call you *Pretzel Girl?*"

Oh my God! Oh my God! He said *Ann.* "Um . . ." How does he know my name? I'm taken off guard. *Say something!* I pick up a pair of white Nikes. "I'm looking for running shoes."

Then I notice the lanyard around his neck. It's flipped backward—again—so I still don't know his name. And we've had too many conversations by now for me to ask him.

"Well, these are men's." He takes them from me and puts them back in the display. "You'll want to look over here." I follow him down the wall, mortified. I can't even tell the difference between men's and women's shoes!

"Are you looking for any certain brand?" he asks.

"No."

"Just running shoes, or cross-trainers?"

I don't know what cross-trainers are. "Just running."

"Don't you want to know how I know your name?"

Huh? What did he say?

Why does this guy keep knocking me off kilter? "Um . . . my name tag?"

He smiles. "You weren't wearing one that first day." I forgot; I didn't get it until the end of the week.

"I was the other day, though."

"No, you weren't." *I wasn't?* Then I remembered that mean guy and my taking it off in the bathroom just before I saw him. He noticed?

"How do you know, then?"

"I asked." He smiles, but softer, shyer than earlier. Is he blushing?

I can't breathe. He asked about me. Who told him? Raynee? Courtney? It doesn't matter. He asked!

After an awkward pause, he says, "So you're a runner?"

I inhale. "Not really." Although right now, my heart is racing like I ran a 5K. Then I realize that sounds stupid. Why would I be looking at running shoes if I'm not a runner? "Well, not yet, anyway."

"Okay. Let's get you started on the right foot." Then he laughs. "Sorry. That was cheesy."

"That's okay." I shift my weight from side to side. I probably look like a little kid who needs to pee. I try to stop. "I like cheese." That was stupid. *I like cheese*, I mock myself. "I mean . . ." What *do* I mean? He waits for me to finish, but I don't know what to say. I grab the nearest shoe—it's hot pink and neon green. "Are these any good?"

"Eh, they're okay, I guess." He picks up a blue pair two shelves over. "These are better."

"Okay. I'll try them."

"What size do you wear?"

"Seven."

A nice, normal size. Respectable. Something I can say out loud. Not like my pants size. Does he believe it? Will he think I'm like Cinderella's stepsisters, who will shove their huge feet into a tiny shoe to impress the prince? *Size seven, please fit. Please fit.*

He disappears into the back and I exhale. I don't think I've taken a full breath since he said he asked about me. *He asked!* My muscles shake like I just did a full workout. Forget Tia and her resistance bands. This is better.

He comes back with two boxes. "I grabbed a half-size bigger, too. They run a little small sometimes."

Small sometimes? They run a little small? Is this his way of saying that he doesn't believe that I, a fat girl, am really a size seven? Is he trying to help me save face? I'm not sure if I'm offended that he doesn't believe me, or if I'm even more in love because he's trying to make me feel better.

"Okay." I sit down on the bench and realize that I am wearing flip-flops. No socks.

He sees that, too. "You can use a pair of these nylon footies." He holds up the box. "Or, if you're sure you're going to buy a pair of shoes, we're running a special where you get a free pack of socks with every shoe purchase. I can open a pack."

Those nylon footie things are disgusting. They sag and make your feet look like nasty old potatoes. No nasty potato feet for me. Cute socks all the way.

"Yeah, I'm planning on buying them," I say. "As long as they fit."

"Let's chance it." He grins and rips open a bag of ankle socks.

He kneels at my feet as he laces up the shoes. Oh my God, he's kneeling at my feet. Like Prince Charming. *Don't giggle.* Am I Cinderella or one of the ugly stepsisters? *Do. Not. Giggle.* Do my feet smell? I had no idea a cute guy would be so close to them when I showered this morning. If I had, I would have paid more attention to them. A giggle tries to escape, but I stifle it and choke on it. It sounds more like a hiccup.

"You okay?" He looks up at me. His eyes scan my face. How many chins do I have at that angle? Can he see up my nose? Oh God, please don't let there be anything up there.

"Uh-huh," I squeak. *Come on, Ann. Get it together. You are just trying on shoes, not losing your virginity.*

He takes my right foot in his hand—correction, cradles my heel in the palm of his hand. So soft. So gentle. The warmth of his hand travels through my heel—oh my God, I can't do this.

I pull my foot out of his hand before he can slip it into the shoe. What kind of freak am I? If I can't handle a guy helping me try on shoes, how will I ever handle something else?

He startles and pulls back.

"Sorry," I say. "My feet are super ticklish."

"No, I'm sorry." He hands me the shoes and stands up. "I didn't mean—"

"It's okay." I shove my feet into the shoes as fast as I can and stand bouncing in them nervously, manically, trying to pretend I'm just testing the fit, but feeling more like I'm going to fly right out of them.

"How do they feel?"

Not as good as your hands, but they'll do.

I walk up and down the aisle. "Great. Thanks."

Size seven. Yes!

"No problem." He puts his hands in the pockets of his black polyester pants. "Hey, are you going to the Knees' Fourth of July party?"

My heart pounds like it's in the middle of Tia's cardio mega-burn section. I lean over to untie the shoes and put them back in the box, trying not to hyperventilate. *Breathe. Slowly. Normally.* Did he just ask me if I'm going to the party? *Inhale.* He couldn't be flirting. *Exhale.* I'm sure he's just making small talk. *Inhale.* He knows I work with them. *Exhale.* That's all. *Stop imagining things, Ann.*

"Um, yeah, I think so." I shove the socks back into the open package and slip my flip-flops back on.

"Cool. I guess I'll see you there, then."

"Yeah. Sure. See you there." I try to nod and act nonchalant, but I feel a stupid grin slide onto my face. I walk away, so I don't just stand there nodding and smiling like a psychopath.

"Hey, Ann," he calls as I pass the soccer equipment.

I turn around. What? Did I forget something?

"Are you on Facebook?"

"Yes." I stare at my flip-flops. Then back up at him, consciously keeping my goofy smile at bay. I feel the sides of my mouth twitching.

"Friend me," he says.

I nod and say, "Okay. Well, see ya. Thanks for the shoes." He didn't actually buy the shoes. He just helped me with them. "I mean, the help. Thanks for helping me."

"No problem."

"Yeah, okay. Bye." Departures alone are reason not to talk to people. They are so awkward. I hate that.

As I pay for my shoes, I go over our conversation in my head again and again. I think of about a thousand cooler things I could have said but didn't. Then I wonder. Was he really interested in seeing me again at the party or was he just making conversation, which is probably part of his job? I'm sure that's it. He was just being a good salesman.

But no matter how hard I try to convince myself that he's nice to all his customers, I can't help but fantasize that maybe, just maybe, he does want to see me again. Then I wonder how I can friend him if I still don't know his name.

27

WHEN I GET HOME, I CONTEMPLATE GOING FOR a run. I decide to download good running songs first. It takes a while.

Then Mom and the twins come home.

I'll run tomorrow.

After she gets dinner in the oven—real semi-homemade lasagna (no-boil noodles and sauce from a jar), the counterpart to my minuscule plastic replica that tastes like dirty sponge and cardboard—Mom puts on "Thriller," and she and the twins practice their moves. I pretend not to watch while I sit at the dining room table with my laptop. I hate to admit it, but there's nothing cuter than seeing Libby and Judd rock out to the funky beat.

I think. *How can I find someone when I don't know his name?* I check Raynee's Facebook page, thinking that maybe I can scroll through her friends. Holy guacamole! She has nearly a thousand! I don't think so. I only work one more shift before the party, and it's by myself, so I send her a message instead.

Then I see her relationship status change—from "single" to "in a relationship." I guess she decided to take Jared back.

Still no message from Tony. He posted a song, but that's it. Cassie's status says she's at tennis camp. I used to miss her like crazy during camp week. Now I don't even know she's gone.

"Hey, Ann." Mom is flushed and panting. "See if there's a 'Thriller' video online somewhere. I can't remember a part and don't want to practice it wrong."

I bring my laptop into the living room, and we all watch it. Then Mom pushes the remote to restart the song and sings along, "It's close to midnight . . ." She poses and claps over her head. Libby and Judd join in.

You know, it looks like fun. I mean, for real.

As if Mom read my mind, she says, "Come on. Join us. Nobody's watching."

At first I wonder how she knows that my problem is that people are watching. Then I remember that she's been my mom all my life. She wrote the notes to get me out of gym class. When she pushed me to play volleyball in middle school, I probably even told her. So her knowing why I shy away from dancing really isn't a secret.

"Yeah, come on, Annie." Libby says without missing a beat.

Come on. Nobody's watching. Yeah, come on. They *want* me to join them. They want me to dance with them. I think about it. I honestly think about it. Who will see? Just Mom and the twins.

Yes, I can do this.

I close my laptop and rise from the couch.

I listen to the rhythm of the music. Feel it.

I'm ready. Ready to groove. Ready to move.

Then the garage door opens and Mike walks in.

"Daddy! Daddy's home!" Libby and Judd run to him and jump on each leg. Even Gigi jumps on him and barks.

"Hey, guys." Mike pulls a familiar cardboard box from a brown paper bag. "Look, Lib. Ice cream. Mint chocolate chip. See? You didn't miss anything the other night. And for the ladies who are watching their figures . . ." Mike shows Mom a container of diet ice cream sandwiches and winks at me.

Mom turns down the music, makes some comment about a rain check and picking this up later, and checks dinner in the oven.

I'm left in the middle of the room. Grooveless.

I transfer my lasagna from the cardboard box to a plate, hoping to trick my brain into thinking it's the same as what everyone else is eating. It might look the same, but it's not. Not even close.

28

I WAKE UP ON THE FOURTH OF JULY EXCITED. NOT only have I lost another three pounds at my scheduled Monday weigh-in, but I lost another half pound today, which brings my total to fourteen and a half! Plus, I'm going to the Knees' party! *I'm going to the Knees' party.* I practically chant it in my head all morning. I skip breakfast and lunch, saving all my calories for party food. I work out with Tia, which I'm able to do all the way through now, some of it high intensity.

During the floor exercises, I think of Dimple Guy. Not knowing his name starts to stress me out. Why hasn't Raynee answered my Facebook message? Should I ask her about it? I don't want her to think I'm pushy, but I'd like to know before I see him—to avoid anything else awkward or embarrassing.

Finding something to wear is even more stressful. It's a pool party, so most of the girls will be wearing swimsuits, mainly bikinis. I wish I had that striped suit I saw with Mom, but it's too late for that now. I opt for some jean shorts and a polo and tank that work with my red and white striped flip-flops, instead.

I might not have as much skin showing as everyone else, but it's the best I can do.

I'm so anxious that I'm ready an hour early. It's a good a thing, too, because Raynee texts and asks me to help her set up. Courtney, Tiffany, and Melanie are still at Courtney's house doing their hair and makeup.

"They want to be fashionably late," Raynee says when I get there, repeating the story nearly in tears. She pulls down a stack of bowls from the top shelf of a kitchen cupboard. "How can you be 'fashionably late' to *your own party*? They do this to me every year. Every year they don't help. Every year I say, 'Never again,' but every year I get sucked into doing it again. Sometimes I think they just use me because I have a pool and my parents let me have parties. And because I'll do all the work. Thank you, thank you, thank you for coming to help. I didn't know who else to call."

"No problem." I help her pour chips into bowls. "I can help clean up later, too, if you want." Actually I'm glad she called. It makes me remember how things used to be with Cassie and me. And makes me realize—for real, even if I did kind of know it for a while—that Cassie and I are not first responders for each other's meltdowns anymore. I knew I missed the hanging out part, but I hadn't thought about missing the helping-out part. Until now.

I want to ask her about what's going on with her and Jared. Are they back together or not? But since she hasn't brought it up, I don't. Maybe it's a touchy subject. "Hey, did you get my Facebook message?" I ask.

"No. Sorry," she says. "This week I've gotten so many messages and friend requests because of the party that I've stopped looking at them." That's a far cry from my one or two a month. "What was it about?"

"I wanted to know—"

"Oh! I almost forgot!" She tears open a bag of M&M's. "Look."

They're red, white, and blue, which isn't surprising. But when I look closer, I see they are personalized: Some say *Knees*. Others *Happy 4th*. Then there are smiley faces. And names: *Rayne, Court, Mel, Tiff*, and—here's the surprising part—some of the M&M's say *Ann* on them.

"What's this?"

"It was your idea, so I added you." She's practically giddy about it. "And it fits, too. Especially if you go by An*nie*."

"Yeah." I'm speechless. Raynee included *me*. As a *Knee*! And everyone who's anyone is going to see. My first Knee party, and I'm not only here, but one of the hostesses. Could today possibly get any better?

We spend the next half hour filling tiki torches with citronella oil; hanging red, white, and blue light strings; and blowing up pool toys with foot pumps.

"Ugh!" Raynee sighs. "People will be here any minute and I'm not even dressed yet."

"It's okay," I tell her. "I can finish this. Go get ready."

"Thanks, Ann. You're the best."

I finish blowing up the pool toys and take the pumps back down to the basement. When I come up the stairs, Courtney, Melanie, and Tiffany are in the kitchen.

"Hey, you guys, look at this." Tiffany's voice. "M&M's. With our names on them."

I wait behind the door, quiet, listening.

"Really?" Someone sounds excited. I think it's Melanie.

"Yeah." Tiffany again. She reads, "Court . . . Tiff—that's me!—Happy Fourth . . ."

"I think they're lame," says Courtney.

"A happy face . . . Here, Mel, this one's yours."

She must have thrown it because Melanie says, "Ow!" just before she says, "Yeah, super lame."

"Oh my God! Look," says Tiffany. "It says, 'Ann.' Who's Ann?"

"She works with me and Raynee, and she's got a thing for my cousin Jon," says Courtney. "I bet she brought these. It was her idea to begin with."

Jon! His name is Jon.

Just as I'm about to open the door, just as I'm about to enter the party, to tell them that Raynee bought them, not me, just then, I hear:

"Does she think she's a Knee now?"

"No freaking way!" says Courtney. "That fat heifer is *not* a Knee!"

I deflate onto the stairs. I cannot open the door. I cannot move. I'm not sure I can breathe. If I could, I would tunnel my way out of this basement and disappear.

From behind the door I hear Raynee's voice. Then Courtney's. Then the doorbell and other voices. And laughter. They're laughing at me. All of them. I know it. I want to die.

29

MY PLAN IS TO WAIT UNTIL EVERYONE GOES OUT
to the pool and slip out through the garage. What was I thinking, coming here in the first place? It takes a while, but eventually
things quiet down enough for me to crack open the door. My heart
pounds in my ears.

I don't see anyone, so I step into the kitchen. Just as Courtney,
of all people, walks in through the sliding glass door from the
patio. She's wearing an American flag bikini top with jean shorts,
and carrying two red plastic cups. "Ann!" She takes a sip. "Where
have you been? The party's outside."

I look at her. Is she serious? Is she really going to pretend that
she likes me?

"Cute shoes!" She hands me one of the cups, puts her arm
around me, and leads me out of the air-conditioning into the
overwhelming heat. Yes, she is. She is pretending we're long-
lost friends. The only way to get away is to make a scene. I don't.
Instead, I go along, fascinated despite myself. What is she up to?

As soon as we get to the pool, she screams, "Let's get this party started!" and everyone whoops and whistles. Melanie plugs her MP3 player into the sound system and cranks it up. Courtney stands on a chaise longue and dances. Melanie and Tiffany join her. All three are wearing American flag bikini tops, but Melanie's shorts are red and Tiffany's are white. Raynee, who is opening a two-liter bottle of pop, wears royal blue shorts. Her bikini top is the same flag pattern, but it's shaped differently. I wonder if she altered it like she did her uniform shirt. Then I wonder if she's as two-faced as Courtney. Has she pretended, too?

I look into my cup—looks like plain pop—and take a sip. I think it's spiked. Is everyone drinking? Raynee never mentioned there'd be alcohol. Maybe it's assumed. I haven't been to a lot of parties. It just surprises me, since her parents are home—making themselves scarce, but still home. I don't want to ask. If I'm wrong, I'll sound paranoid. If I'm right, then I'll sound lame. Since there's probably about a thousand calories in every sip, not to mention that I've never had anything besides the occasional glass of wine at family functions, I'll just pretend to drink it.

I take another tiny sip, sit at a metal umbrella table, and look around. Jared Dunne and Raynee are talking by the food table and seem pretty intense. Are they breaking up or getting back together? I can't tell.

Practically everyone who's anyone is here. The football players. The cheerleaders. The entire student government. All mingling together. All way cooler than me. I'm starting to sweat.

"Hey, Ann!" Naomi scrapes a black metal chair across the cement pool area and sits next to me. She's wearing a metallic silver bikini. Is it the one she bought at Keehn's or from *Vicky's*? It looks like Snapz! "Thanks for babysitting the monster the other night."

"Uh-huh." I sip. It's not like I knew what I was getting into, but I don't say that.

"If you hadn't stepped up, your dickhead dad would've made me do it." She pops an M&M in her mouth. I wonder if it says *Ann*.

Dickhead? She's not talking about *my dad* like that, is she? Is she really? It's one thing for Uncle Doug and Mom to call him that. But Naomi?

"Yeah," she continues, "you're so lucky you don't have to live with him. He's such a dick."

Lucky? What is she talking about? Somehow I have never considered it lucky that my dad did the bare minimum required by the courts to take responsibility for me and my brother while he did *everything* for Nancy's kids. I would've given anything to have him around more. Anything. Besides, it's *her mother* who's the lunatic, not my dad.

I take a swig of liquid courage and ask, "Lucky?"

"Hell yeah," she says. "Living in that house is a nightmare. Constant yelling and screaming. Do you have any idea how many times your dad has cheated on my mom?"

"Cheated? My dad? No way!" I gulp now. It's getting smoother the more I drink. Has she ever met my dad? He's totally devoted to Nancy. Isn't he?

Tristan Todd throws some girl into the pool, but she holds on and he falls, too. Water splashes everywhere, including some in my drink. Naomi covers hers with her hand. Everyone cheers and claps.

"Yes way." She chugs from her cup—one, two, three big swallows. Man, she's hardcore. Maybe hers isn't as strong as mine. Or maybe she's used to drinking more than I am. "He even knocked up his ex-administrative assistant. He was about to leave Mom for her when Mom got preggers with Noah."

"Lynn? No way! How do you *know* all of this?"

"I told you. They yell constantly. You can't be in that house and not know. He screams. Mom screams. Noah screams, too."

I heard Noah scream firsthand, but I figured it was because he didn't know me. This is too much. Naomi must be drunk or something. I don't think I've ever heard Dad and Nancy fight. Maybe a little, but nothing major.

I polish off the rest of my drink, and, like a waiter at some of the fancy places Mike takes us, Tiffany brings me another one.

I sip at it as the music gets louder and more and more people pack around the pool. Naomi leans in closer, practically yelling above the noise. "Mom is so stressed out that he's going to leave her for Lynn, even though she miscarried. That's why she drags us all to church. Hoping that if he can get religion, too, he'll straighten up. But he just uses church to get more business connections. And he's probably checking out women *there*, too."

I'm not sure what my face looks like, but I must seem pretty stunned, because then she says, "Don't tell me you didn't know. He cheated on your mom, too. That's why she kicked him out. That's how he ended up with *my* mom. Only she claims she didn't know he was married until after your mom caught him. By then she *loved* him." She says *loved* like it's a dirty word.

I guess I knew he cheated on Mom, but I always figured *he* left *her*. And that Mom pushed him to it because she's so anal and intense. I never thought about it being the other way around. And why didn't I? It's not like he's been the model father or anything. Why did I just *assume* it was *all* mom?

"Did Tony know?" I take a long gulp. .

"I don't know what he knew," she says, "but he sure knew enough to get shit started. It was because of Tony that Nate and I started asking questions. It's really sickening. God, Ann. I thought you knew. I figured that's why you stayed away from the nuthouse. I've been so embarrassed by it that I can hardly look at you."

"Why?"

"You don't have to live there. *Your* family is normal." She downs the rest of her drink. "I'm going to get some more. Want some?"

I look into my nearly empty cup. My head spins, and I'm not sure if it's from the drink, the techno music—how long has that been playing?—or from what I've heard. This whole day has been so bizarre. I'm at a Knee party. A freaking Knee party! Even though at least one of them thinks I'm a fat cow. Probably all of them. And I am, which is even more depressing.

Then I find out that Naomi, who I thought hated me, really just hates my dad. My dickhead dad, who I didn't even know was a dickhead before today. Well, somewhat, but not this much.

And this whole idea of *her* family and *my* family. Is *my* dad part of *her* family? Shouldn't *he* be part of *mine*, dickhead or not? The funny part is that I don't feel like either family is *my* family. One is Mike and Mom's. One is Dad and Godzilla's. My family is pieces and parts. Kind of like Mondo Burger chicken nuggets.

To top it all off, I think I'm getting drunk. And I don't even care. Not one bit.

30

TWO—OR IS IT THREE—DRINKS LATER, "THRILLER" comes on. Shrill screams from the Knees practically burst my eardrum. Or is that me screaming? I'm not sure. I'm not sure about anything right now, except that I can't feel my nose. It's numb. I keep touching it to see if it's still there. I feel warm all over. And it's amazing how much I don't care about anything. I don't care about the wedding. Or dresses. Or diets. I don't care about Courtney. Or Naomi. Or dickhead dads. I don't care about not caring. I love it. Maybe I'll start drinking every day. Screw the calories.

A few people start doing the Thriller. "I know that dance," I say to the girl next to me. She was in my algebra class last year. Can't remember her name.

"Go do it, then," she says.

"Maybe I will."

I stagger to the dance area and wait for the exact right moment. The next thing I know I'm moving, dancing. And singing.

Except I'm in public and this person dancing is not me.

It's dream me. The me of my imagination.

The outgoing, not-fat, not-embarrassed, not-worried-about-what-people-think me. Nobody can see me. I'm invisible. Even to myself.

I only feel me. Sliding and grooving and stepping and clapping and Thriller clawing my way across the pool patio under the red, white, and blue party lights. The music moves through me and moves me like a puppeteer. Like Michael Jackson himself is holding the strings. Like I'm part of this big group—Knees and athletes and smart kids and not-so-smart kids—all bonded together by the red cups. One big mass of cups Thriller-ing together.

Then the music stops, and I realize that I've had my eyes closed. When I open them, there's Courtney, staring at me and smiling. A huge, evil grin. Melanie and Tiffany are next to her, and it's obvious they've been watching me for a while.

Watching. Me. For a while.

There is space all around me. Nobody else is dancing. Nobody else is as drunk as me. I can tell because they're all looking at me like I'm an alien. They are just standing around, talking and eating. When did they stop dancing? How long have I been dancing by myself? A few seconds? Minutes? The whole time? It doesn't matter. I look like a complete idiot.

My face burns. I have to get out of here. I need to get home. I need to relocate to a foreign country. I weave through the crowd headed toward the garage, my gateway to freedom, when out of nowhere Dimple Guy—*Jon*—is right in front of me.

"Hi." He smiles. Those dimples! He's even cuter than I remember. So cute that I forget where I'm going. He must have recently showered because he smells like soap. And some kind of cologne.

"How are the new shoes?"

"Fine." I don't tell him that they are still in the box. Or that I'm dizzy.

My stomach churns. I remember that I haven't eaten anything today. The first day in my whole stinking life that I don't eat happens to be the first day in my whole stinking life that I drink. What are the odds? With me, there are no odds. It's a given.

I need to sit down, so I sit on the edge of the pool and stick my feet in, flip-flops and all.

He sits facing me. "Are you okay?"

"Fine."

"You still haven't friended me."

"I will." My eyelids are really heavy. "I promise. Now that I know your name."

He laughs.

"What? Your name tag is always backward." I move my feet in the water and watch the ripples.

He laughs again and puts his hand on my arm. "I'm sorry. If I'd known, I would have introduced myself."

"It's okay." I look at him and consciously open my eyes, so I don't look as out of it as I feel. "I should have asked." He asked, I remember, and I can't help but smile.

"You have the bluest eyes," he says.

"Thank you." My face is hot. Even hotter than earlier.

"I saw you dancing," he says. "You're really good."

Dancing! Now I remember. I was leaving. I stand up and almost fall. Jon stands, too, and steadies me. "I've got to go."

"Go? Go where?" He's holds my shoulders and looks straight into my eyes. I want to kiss him. "Are you okay? Have you been drinking?"

I close my eyes again. Everything is spinning. My stomach churns.

"Ann?"

I open my eyes. I know Jon is talking to me. He just asked me something. I want to answer. I open my mouth to say something, something cool, but instead I hurl nasty-tasting brown liquid all over Jon's used-to-be pure white and clean Nikes.

31

I WAKE UP ON THE FLOOR OF RAYNEE'S BEDROOM covered with a purple and gray fuzzy blanket. It freaks me out at first because I don't expect to be there. I bolt upright and see Raynee asleep in her bed.

My head kills, and my mouth feels furry and tastes putrid. Have I been licking her floor in my sleep or what? Gross. My stomach is queasy, and I suddenly remember retching my guts out most of the night.

I remember Raynee rescuing me. Taking me from Jon and his pukey shoes and all the staring, snickering can-hold-their-alcohol cool kids. Putting me in the bathroom with a plastic basin and a wet washcloth. Giving me water, Motrin, and a clean T-shirt. Telling her parents that I ate something bad for lunch—she thinks a hot dog from the gas station. "Ah," says her mother, "that'll do it. Poor thing. Should we call her parents?"

Raynee texted Mom from my phone, "Having fun. OK if I spend the night at Raynee's?" I remember feeling relieved when Mom texted back, "Sure. See you tomorrow. ☺" Then Raynee ran interference for hours when people wanted to get in the bathroom or asked what happened. She probably cleaned up all by herself; I was in no condition to help. But I'd told her I would. What kind of friend am I? No wonder Cassie dumped me.

I lie back down and wait for Raynee to wake up. Besides, the stiller I am the better I feel.

Then, as every gory detail from the party flashes through my pounding head, I decide not to wait. I don't want to face Raynee. She must be so pissed at me. She should be. I ruined her party. *I'm* pissed at me.

Even though I try to be quiet, I end up creaking the floor and rustling blankets trying to find my purse and flip-flops. My shirt is draped over a chair, freshly washed.

"Hey," says Raynee. "How are you feeling?"

"I'm sorry to wake you up." I stand awkwardly in the middle of her room.

"It's fine. I was worried about you."

"I'm sorry, Raynee. I'm so sorry. I ruined your party. I'm so sorry. Did I say I'm sorry? Because I am."

She laughs. "You didn't ruin anything. Courtney did. She's the one who spiked your drinks all night."

"Yeah, so? Didn't she spike everyone's?"

"No." Raynee sits cross-legged on her bed. She makes room for me. I lean against the cool wall. "You see, Tiffany always gets a bottle of something to spike drinks with. Because it's small, everyone gets a little and nothing gets out of hand. But Court convinced Tiff that it would be funny to give it all to you. That watching you get smashed would be more fun than all of us getting a little buzzed."

"Why me? And why are you telling me this? Aren't they your best friends?"

Raynee takes a deep breath. "Because it's my fault they did this. I bought the M&M's. I didn't talk to them about adding your name. I didn't think they'd mind. Well, they did. They thought you bought them and were trying to push your way into our group."

"I know that part. I heard them." Then I tell her what happened, skipping the fat cow part.

"Well, I had no idea. I was so busy keeping chip bowls filled, getting out more pop, and arguing with Jared that—"

"I saw that," I jump in. I've been wondering and waiting for the opportunity. "Everything okay with you two?"

"Everything's okay with *me*. *You two* no longer applies to us. We're done. This time for good." Raynee seems resolved, but only time will tell. "Anyway, I didn't notice what they were doing." She changes the subject. "Not until 'Thriller.'"

"Ugh!" I cover my face and knock my head into the wall. "Don't remind me!"

"That was when I started asking questions. Melanie told me everything. She feels bad, too, but she'd never stand up to Courtney."

"That makes more sense, I guess. But what about Naomi? Was she in on it?" Was the stuff she said true or just a distraction to keep me drinking?

"I don't know," Raynee says. "Courtney and Naomi are friends, but Melanie didn't mention her." It wouldn't surprise me. I should've known something was up when she was suddenly all chummy with me. But who knows, maybe everything she said is true.

I'm confused.

All I know is that I feel like shit and I'm exhausted. I just want to go home, crawl into bed, and disappear.

"Thanks for everything." I look at the shirt I'm wearing. It's from a 5K run. "And for not making me sleep in a pukey shirt. Do you want it back now, or should I wash it first?"

"It used to be my dad's, but now I sleep in it." She drops back onto her pillow. "It's up to you."

I tell her I'll wash it and return it the next time I see her. I thank her again and head home. On the way, I think about Jon. I'm not convinced he was ever interested in me. But even if he was, he isn't now. Nothing is more of a turn-off than someone puking on your shoes.

My life hasn't been wonderful, but now it's crossed into disaster. At least there's comfort in knowing that it couldn't possibly get any worse.

I get a text but don't check it until I pull in the driveway. It's from Cassie. *You went to the Knees' party without me?*

I text back. *Been meaning to tell you. How did you know?*

I peel off my clothes and jump in the shower. When I get out, my phone is blinking. *It's all over FB. You know the Thriller?*

Oh my God. Oh my God. Still wrapped in a towel, I grab my laptop and pull up Facebook. Right on my page is a picture of me dancing! I look as deranged as I imagined. Maybe even worse. I feel like I'm going to vomit, again.

Then I realize that I don't have to search to find and friend Jon. He's tagged in the freaking picture, and so are all four of the Knees! Jon Reilly. His last name is Reilly. I remove my tag and delete it from my timeline, but since I didn't post it—I don't even know the person who did—I can't remove it completely. I pray that nobody in my family saw it.

I send Jon a friend request, but I fully expect him to decline it. After all, he reminded me *before* I threw up on him. He has over 800 friends, including Cassie—turns out they go to the same school. Everybody knows everybody in this town.

I get a notification for a friend request. Actually, I have twenty-three! If only these people wanted to be my friend legitimately, instead of just to laugh at me. So much for being in on the Fourth of July party jokes—I *am* the joke.

32

I SPEND THE NEXT FEW DAYS AROUND THE HOUSE, doing laundry, avoiding seeing anyone who might have been at the party. Avoiding anything to do with dancing, like Tuesday night lessons. The worst part about being a girl is cramps, but sometimes they come in handy.

Nobody in the family has said anything, so I assume that I removed the photo from my timeline early enough. I keep getting friend requests, though, so it's still out there.

I weigh myself and find that half pound I lost on the Fourth. A gain!

I think I'm the only person in the world to gain half a pound after spending a night puking. Up. Down. Up. Down. It's not a weight loss roller coaster. Roller coasters are fun. So are yo-yos. This is not entertaining and not a game. This is torture. Like playing with a Red Ryder BB gun and actually shooting your eye out.

Even though I've lost fourteen pounds, I still have so far to go.

That afternoon, I am scheduled to work—with Courtney, no

less. I don't want to look at Courtney, let alone spend six hours with her. I'm sure the feeling is mutual. I would call in sick, but there is no way I'm uttering the word *cramps* or anything remotely related to it to Mr. D—ski. Maybe Courtney will call in.

No such luck. She's already there when I arrive.

She moonwalks across the floor and sings "Thriller." Only she doesn't know the words, so she just mimics the beat. Then she cracks up.

I shoot her a look and put on my apron. This is going to be a long day. I'd love to tell her off. But what good will it do? I knew not to trust her. I knew the drink was spiked. I could taste it. I was the one who kept drinking. I was the one who made a fool of myself. It was me. Sure, she's slime. Sure, I hate her. But still.

The back door opens and in walks Raynee. "Hey, what are you doing here?" asks Courtney.

"Mr. D—ski called me," she says. "He asked me to meet him here."

"That's weird."

Right then Mr. D. shows up. Before he says a single word, he sighs about a thousand times. "Thanks for coming in on your day off, Raynee." He sighs again.

"No problem." Raynee glances at me, asking me with her eyes what I know. I shrug slightly. I have no idea what's going on.

"First off, I got a report from a customer about Ann." He looks at me. "He says he waited ten minutes for someone to come to the counter, and when you did, you told him he needed to wait another ten for a pretzel?"

My heart is racing. Am I going to get fired? Should I tell him everything? Courtney watches me. I could throw her under the bus so easily—and she knows it. She was on the phone. The warmer was empty when I got here. And on and on.

"It was a bad day. I burned my hand and dropped a tray of pretzels. And there was a rush—"

"Did you fill out an accident form?" he asks. "And report the pretzel loss?"

"No, sir," I say. "I didn't know we needed to. Or how to."

"I'll show you how to do that before I leave," he says, and pulls a clipboard from his briefcase. Does that mean he's not firing me? That's good. Maybe this is *strike one*—like baseball, three strikes and you're out.

Then he starts sighing again. "I hate this part of my job." Another sigh. "Hate it."

What part? Is there more? I fidget, first picking at my nails, then putting my hands in my pants pocket and rocking back and forth, then picking my nails again. What did I do or *not* do now? Why doesn't he just get to the point?

"I'm sure you're wondering what's going on, so I'll just get to the point." Another sigh. "I'm sure you're aware that we keep monthly reports of the cup and pretzel consumption at each store."

I didn't know about the reports, but I knew they kept track. He told me that when he hired me. That's why he gave me the plastic cup.

"Well, there was a pretty large discrepancy this past month between the amount of cups and pretzels ordered and the money in the register and credit card receipts."

What? Is he accusing us of stealing from the register?

"I want to give you the benefit of the doubt." He looks at each of us, one at a time, right in the eye. I squirm. Not because I did anything wrong but because he's staring at me and thinks I did something. I know he does. After all, the other report was about me. "Was there an accident involving cups? A damaged case? Something you should have reported and didn't?"

I shake my head. I look at Raynee and Courtney. They look as stunned as I do. "Not that I know of," says Raynee. "Court?"

"No," she says. "If any cases came in with problems, I would immediately report it. Immediately."

"Okay, then." He sighs. "Somebody's been stealing."

After we all deny taking money from the register, he clarifies. "I'm not saying it's from the register. It could be consuming more than your daily allotment of one pretzel and an occasional paper cup, or giving away food and drinks to your friends. The discrepancy is much larger than one unreported tray."

Like Gigi squirming under the bed when Mom is on a rampage, Courtney covers herself. "I never eat while I'm at work. I don't even like pretzels." Then she adds, "No offense."

"None taken," says Mr. D.

She's such a liar. I open my mouth to call her on it, but before any words come out, Courtney adds, "But Ann does. She eats pretzels all the time. With cheese. And uses cups, too." She looks at me. "Sorry, Ann. We're friends, and I hate telling on you, but I just can't lie."

Oh my God! Why would she do that? Especially after I kept my mouth shut about her.

"I do not! *You* do!" I know as I say it that it sounds more like retaliation than truth. But it is the truth. It is! I feel my face flush. I take deep breaths. "And *you're* the one who gives away stuff, too."

"Yeah?" Courtney looks so smug I could slap her. "To who?"

"To Naomi, for one! And the people in line waiting for pretzels."

"I was trying to keep the customers from walking away after *you* dropped the pretzels. And you mean Naomi, *your* stepsister? I think you might be mistaking me with, um, I don't know . . . you." What did I ever do to her? Up until I started working here, Courtney barely gave me the time of day. Now I'm her worst enemy.

"Okay," says Mr. D. "That's enough. Raynee, do you know anything about this? Have you seen either Courtney or Ann give food away to anyone? *Naomi*, perhaps?"

"Actually, sir." Raynee's voice cracks. "I didn't see anything. Naomi is Ann's stepsister, but—"

"See?" says Courtney.

Strike two.

"But I didn't see anything," Raynee continues. "I'm sorry. And as far as eating, I know that I eat pretzels sometimes, and I've forgotten my plastic cup and used paper ones."

"We allow for a certain amount of that," says Mr. D. "I'm looking for excessive abuses."

"I don't know," says Raynee.

"You know," says Courtney, as sweet as Coke. Spiked Coke. Putrid puked spiked Coke. "Ann might not even know she's doing it. I saw on TV the other day how so many Americans eat without paying attention—"

"Shut up, Courtney!" I scream, rage pounding in my ears. "Just shut the hell up!"

"Miss Galardi, please!" Mr. D. breaks in. "That's enough."

Strike three. I'm out.

"Yes, it is." I pull off my apron and throw it onto the counter. This is bullshit. "I'm sorry. I've got to go."

Then I walk straight out the back door and to my car.

I can't believe this. I didn't do anything. Some guy reports me because of Courtney's laziness. Then they think I stole food because I'm the fattest? I didn't steal a morsel. Not one single thing. I didn't even eat any pretzels. I didn't have any nacho cheese. I brought my plastic cup every day I was there. I want to scream, but instead I break down in tears. My one small victory: Courtney doesn't see me cry.

33

A MONDO BURGER BILLBOARD TAUNTS ME through my tears on the way home. A Mega Mondo Combo Meal and a Coke. The way the condensation of the side of the Coke cup glistens is almost pornographic. I swear the sesame seed bun and the finely chopped onions peeking out with the pickles between the ketchup and onions are talking to me. *You know you want me.* The fries are golden perfection.

It's all fake. I know it. The real fries at Mondo Burger have probably been sitting under the heat lamps for a while and are rubbery and gross. I do not want a Mondo Burger. I've struggled to lose fourteen pounds. Just looking at the billboard threatens to put a quarter pound on my thighs.

But that picture burns into my brain. I imagine biting into the hot, juicy burger, the medley of taste and texture harmonizing with the fries and icy Coke. That seductive Coke. That's all I can think about. I push everything else aside—Courtney, Mr. Dumbass-ski, fatness, and bridesmaids' dresses.

As if I'm following the orders of the Mondo Burger marketing team, I turn the wheel and pull up to the drive-through. I order a Mega Mondo Combo Meal with a Coke. Make that *Diet Coke*. And then add an order of chicken nuggets with sweet mustard sauce, which takes my total to $6.45. All I have is a five, so I dig around for the other $1.45 in various small coins, including nearly twenty pennies. I know the Mondo dude is annoyed, but I don't care. At least I tell myself I don't care. Actually, I'm super-embarrassed that I ordered so much and have to scrape the bottom of the ash-tray to pay for it. Like I'm desperate. Which I am. Which I hate.

After I get the food and check the bag because they always forget something—and have to ask for sweet mustard because they forgot it, of course—I pull over into a parking space and stuff my face with Mondo crap.

There's no need to rush and little risk of anyone seeing me, but I eat like I'm racing the clock. Like if I stop, something will catch me. I barely taste it, which sucks because there have been so many S2S nights where my stomach is growling and I dream all night about a Mondo Burger Combo. I want to taste it, savor it, enjoy it. Like in my dreams.

But no.

Instead I shove more food in my mouth before I swallow the previous bite. I catch a glimpse of my face in the side mirror. There is ketchup on my cheek, which is puffed out like a chipmunk— fatter than usual—making me feel like a vampire who has just devoured a chipmunk.

Mascara streaks down my face from crying. A stray fry has fallen onto my chest, waiting to be noticed. I'm surprised it escaped. I brush off the crumbs, wipe my face, and dispose of the secret paper carcass of my kill. All but the Coke. It is diet, after all.

When I get home, Mom is there, which surprises me since it's the middle of the day. She is scrubbing the kitchen floor. "Why are you home?"

"Nice to see you, too." She sits up and back on her heels. "I live here."

"Very funny."

"Donna has a doctor's appointment this afternoon, so I didn't have anyone to watch the kids."

"What about me?" I sip from the Mega Mondo cup.

"I thought you had to work." She drops the sponge into the bucket of sudsy water. "So why are *you* home? And what's with the Mondo cup?"

"It's diet, for your information." I try to sound offended.

I don't mention the Mega Mondo Combo that it was attached to. I don't mention work, either.

I'm not sure if it's pop fizz or guilt, but suddenly I feel like I could puke all over Mom's clean floor. Purge all the Mondo grease that is coating my gut right now. All the things that Courtney said and did. Everything. I want to tell her everything. But if I do, will she believe me? Will she take my side? Or will she see through my Mondo lie and think I stole Twisted Pretzel stuff, too? After all, why wouldn't the fat girl steal food? She lies about it. She hides it. She gorges herself on it.

"Mommy." Judd stands on the carpet right where it meets the oak flooring. "I'm hungry."

"Just a minute." Mom holds her hand up like a cartoon cop at an intersection. "I'm almost done here, and then I'll get you something."

"But I want something now." He holds his stomach like he's

178

wasting away. Then he flashes the cute, sly smile that always wins her over. "Just a little bitty cookie, maybe?"

I laugh at his drama and appreciate the diversion that allows me to slip upstairs. Halfway up, I hear Mom relent.

I knew it.

When I go to my room, I see my new running shoes peeking out of the box. I should go for a run and work off the Mondo calories.

It's cloudy. Might rain. I'll run tomorrow.

34

LIBBY'S ROOM, WHICH USED TO BE TONY'S, IS NEXT
to mine. I can hear her talking to herself as I head for the bathroom. Normally, I don't pay much attention, but I hear the word
fat and stop outside her door. And listen.

"No, Teddy," she scolds. "No more cake for you. You are too fat
already."

I peek around the corner. She has her dolls and stuffed animals
arranged around her play table with teacups and plates at each
place. She stands at her play kitchen, tiara on her head and blue
princess dress-up gown over her clothes.

"Want some cake?" she asks a doll. She waits a moment, as if
the doll is saying something. "No, I'm not having any. I am too fat.
I can't eat cake. I am going to be a flower girl in Aunt Jackie's wedding. I have to be on a diet. That's what you do. You don't eat food.
You say, 'No, no, I couldn't eat another bite.'

"Then you stand on that thing by the shower and say, 'I'm so
fat. I need to go on a diet.' Then you stand in front of the mirror
and do this." Libby sucks in her cheeks, making fish lips, and then

she sucks in her belly until her ribs stick out. "Then after you get dressed, you ask Daddy if the outfit makes you look fat." She twirls around in the dress.

Then: "Teddy, are you paying attention to me? This is very, very important." She shakes her finger at poor Teddy. "Eating too much food makes you cry. You only eat when nobody is watching. Then nobody will see you get fat. That's what Annie does. Or you run and run and run the fat away. That's what Mommy does. And you yell a lot. That makes fat go away, too. That's why I yell at you, Teddy. So I can help you not get fat."

Eating too much food makes you cry. So I can help you not get fat. Her words echo in my head. I remember that day after dance class in the van. When Mom yelled about helping me and my wanting ice cream. Libby was in the backseat.

What else does she see?

A lot, apparently.

What the hell are we doing to her?

I feel sick to my stomach. And not because I ate practically a whole farm—a processed, extruded farm—either. I've spent so much time thinking about what Mom says and does and how it has affected me and my weight, but never once did I think about Libby, about her living in this house with perfect Mom and imperfect me, both of us complaining about our weight all the time. The mixed-up, messed-up messages she's getting.

She sits down at the table with her little dolls and animals, pours them pretend tea, and drinks hers with her pinky out. How does she know to do that? She looks so innocent. So sweet. So small. Most of the time I see her as annoying. But she's my sister. My little sister. Don't I owe it to her to not mess her up? I suddenly feel racked with guilt. For not being a good role model. A good sister. A good person.

I go into the room. "Hey, Lib. Whatcha doing?"

"Playing tea party." She pours herself some more "tea." "Do you want to play?"

"Sure." I plop cross-legged on the floor next to the table.

She hands me an empty plate. "Would you like some cake?"

I pretend to take a little piece. "Yes, please. Just a little though. Cake tastes good, but too much isn't healthy."

And just like that, I have a new plan: To show Libby that weight and looks are not what matters. I want her to be healthy, not screwed up. I'll do whatever I can, even if I have to fake it.

35

THE FIRST HURDLE IN OPERATION HEALTHY LIBBY IS cancelling S2S. I still can't find the CANCEL AUTO-SHIP checkbox, so I'm calling customer service.

Eating shouldn't be a punishment, and doing this program feels like one. Like I'm beating myself up for being overweight. I hate the food, so I don't think it would work in the long run, anyway. I dream constantly of living life like a normal person once I get to my ideal weight. Why can't I learn to live like a normal person by living like one now? It's so obvious that I can't believe I haven't thought of it before.

After going through a long series of automated prompts, which I have to repeat twice to find an option to speak to a real person, I wait on hold for over a half an hour, listening to the same recorded promo loop over and over and over. Finally, someone answers. "Thank you for calling Secrets 2 Success. This is Jasmine. May I have your customer ID?" I tell her, and then she has me verify my shipping address and phone number. "How may I assist you today?"

"I'd like to cancel auto-ship."

"Oh?" she says. "May I ask why?"

"I don't like the food."

"Did you know that you can tailor the program to fit your tastes? Simply log on to your account and—"

"Yes, I know," I say. Why can't she just do what I want? "I don't like *any* of the food. I just want to cancel."

"You can change your auto-ship options by logging on—"

"No! You can't!" I yell. Then I calm myself and start again. "I've already tried that twice. Could you cancel it for me, please?"

"One moment while I transfer you to a program consultant."

"No, Jasmine, wait!" But I'm too late. Another promo loop. Another five minutes.

Finally, another person—Cindy—answers, and I not only have to repeat my customer ID, address, and phone number but also go through the same kind of "why I want to cancel" conversation. Then Cindy says, "Statistics show that when people stop following a balanced diet and exercise program—like the Secrets 2 Success Weight Loss System—they gain an average of five pounds per month. Are you sure you want—"

"Yes!" I snap. "Can I just cancel my auto-ship?" I'm on the verge of tears. "*Please?*"

Finally Cindy agrees to do it, but it takes another ten minutes. I take slow, even breaths to keep from melting down. After I hang up, I vow to never buy anything I see on an infomercial again.

Sprawled out on my bed, I'm relieved. S2S is over. And, I realize, it's the second time today I've stood up for myself.

Next hurdle: Mom.

As if on cue, she calls us all for dinner. Mike grilled marinated chicken breasts and Mom made a huge salad with strawberries, walnuts, and a ton of veggies—greens, cucumber, celery, red bell pepper, onion, and baby Portobello mushrooms. Her dinner is so perfect I could kiss her. But I don't.

We all flock to the table like vultures. The first thing Judd always does when we have chicken is sing, "Chicky chicky bawk bawk, chicky chicky bawk. Chicky chicky bawk bawk, chicky chicky bawk." I want to tell him to cool it, but he amuses Mike so much that the last time I said anything, Mom yelled at me for like an hour.

Since Mom found out about S2S, I've eaten with the fam. I nuke a dinner while she gets their dinner on the table. Tonight I sit down and dish regular food onto my plate. Regular food! Not pre-packaged, taste-removed stuff. Mom shoots me a confused, somewhat annoyed look. One that I'm sure she expects me to address. I don't.

"Where's your dinner, Ann?" asks Judd.

"Right here." I put the tongs back into the salad bowl. "I'm having what you're having."

Mom puts salad onto Libby's plate. "I hate salad. It's so leafy," Libby says.

"Not me," I put a forkful into my mouth. "I love it. It's yummy and pretty, too."

Mom and Mike look at me and then at each other. Mom mouths "yummy?" and Mike mouths "pretty?" and raises his eyebrows. It's all I can do to keep from laughing.

Libby watches me for a second, takes a bite and then another. Then Mom looks at me, even more confused. I kind of like not being predictable. Mixing things up a little. Being surprising. Like Tony, without the tension.

I eat one piece of chicken and a pile of salad without saying a word.

Just smirking.

Like I'm up to something.

Which I am.

We're nearly done when the doorbell rings. "I'll get it." Judd is at the door before anyone can object. "Ann, it's for you," he says. "Her name's Raynee."

Raynee? I wonder what she wants.

When I stand up, there's still some food left on my plate. "I'm done," I say, proud of myself. *Slimmer You* says, "Leave a few bites on your plate. It signals the brain that you are full with some food to spare and reduces the need for seconds." I've read that tip nearly a hundred times, but I've never actually done it before. It feels nice to walk away. Sure, it *is* because Raynee is here, but still.

"Don't you want dessert?" asks Libby. "Mommy made pineapple cookies."

"Go ahead without me." I take my plate to the dishwasher. "I had cake earlier—at the tea party—remember?"

Libby smiles.

"Tea party?" Mom asks.

"Ann and me had a tea party today with Teddy and my babies."

I meet Raynee at the door, leaving Mom and Mike confused—and probably a little suspicious—and Libby babbling on about the party.

"Hey." I invite Raynee in and take her to my room where we can talk.

"Hey," she says on the way upstairs. "I wasn't sure if you'd see me. You were pretty upset earlier."

"Yeah, well, how would you feel? I didn't take anything."

"I know," she says. "I know, and I told Mr. D—ski that when you left."

"You did?" I close the door and kick a pile of clothes away from my desk so Raynee can move out the chair. Then I sit on my bed and lean into my pillows.

"Yes, I did." She doesn't say anything about my room being a mess—hers was, too, kind of—and leans back in the chair. "I didn't see anyone give anything to Naomi, so I couldn't speak to that, but I did tell what I saw. You know, how Courtney always forgot her plastic cup and used paper ones for drinks and nacho cheese. How she ate more pretzels than you and me combined. And how it wouldn't surprise me one bit if she gave stuff to her friends, but it would shock me senseless if you did."

I sit straight up. No way. "You said all that?"

"Had to," she says. "What Courtney's been doing is wrong. I should have done something sooner."

"Wow . . ." I'm stunned. "Thanks."

"She wasn't always like this—just so you know. I have better taste in friends than that."

"I can't imagine how she reacted when you started talking."

"Let's just say that Courtney and I are no longer friends. She says I'm not a Knee anymore—that once she tells Mel and Tiff about my getting her fired, they'll be on her side."

"Fired?" Wait! *Courtney* got fired? And now Raynee might have lost her friends—because of me.

"She's probably right, too. Tiffany practically worships her. I don't need to be a Knee. Not if it means being mean. I'm not like that. I guess I'm not Ray*nee* anymore, just Rayne." She kind of smiles.

"Aw, man. I'm sorry."

"It's okay. Really. And yeah, she got fired, and Mr. D. said you could have your job back if you wanted it. He understood why you left. And don't be sorry." Raynee slips off her flip-flops and rests her feet on my bed rails. Makes herself comfortable. Like an old friend, not someone at my house for the first time. "I'm tired of Courtney's crap."

"Yeah." I'm not sure what I'm agreeing with. I guess I'm just amazed. Nobody has ever done anything like this for me before. Nobody. Ever. Not even Cassie.

"I knew you would understand." Raynee picks at a spot of purple nail polish on the side of her big toe. "You were friends with that Cassie girl."

"Huh?" What does she mean by "that Cassie girl"?

Raynee looks embarrassed. "I'm sorry. Are you two still close? I shouldn't've said anything."

"No, we're not. It's okay. What about her?"

"I don't know." She backtracks. Like she's afraid to talk bad about Cassie. "It's just, you know . . ."

"No . . ." I lean in. "Tell me. Please."

"I just know that a lot of people didn't like her when she went to our school. She was so pushy and bossy. And loud. And obnoxious. I guess I just avoided you, too, because you guys seemed like a package deal. I'm glad you're not, though."

I knew how Cassie was, but I still thought people liked her. Probably because I liked her. At least I did until I got some distance from her, and I met Raynee, who is the complete opposite of Cassie. All this time I thought I missed my best friend. Maybe I've missed what a best friend is.

I'm used to people telling me what to do and then moving on, choosing other things over me. Cassie. My parents. And Tony, too. I'm used to rejection. What I'm not used to is people choosing me. Me over everyone else. What I'm not used to is feeling special.

"Hey, have you seen your photo lately?" she says.

"It's not exactly *my* photo." I flop back and bury my face in my pillow.

Raynee hands me my laptop. "Check it out. You've got a ton of 'likes.'"

I'm reluctant. I don't really want to see it again. Except I can't. It's not there anymore. I check Jon's page to see if it's there, which it isn't. My friend request is still pending. Proof that he doesn't want anything to do with me.

Raynee tries to find it, too, but it's gone. Removed. "That's weird. It was there yesterday."

I pull her shirt out of my laundry basket. "Sorry it's not folded," I say as I hand it to her, "but it's clean."

She sets my laptop on the bed and takes the shirt. "No problem." When she stands up, she accidentally kicks one of my funky Converse Chuck Taylor low-tops. "Ooh, these are cute!" She picks it up and looks at the size. "Ugh. My clodhoppers won't fit. Too bad, too, because you have such adorable shoes." Then she laughs. "Not like I'm trying to steal them or anything."

I say, "I know," and laugh, too. What I don't tell her is that I'm thrilled that she'd even think about borrowing my shoes. Something good friends do.

36

SLIMMER YOU SAYS, "DON'T PROCRASTINATE. Don't wait until Monday. Start living healthy today." Too late. I've already put off working out with Tia since before the party. Put off running for over a week. Put off being healthy most of my life.

Green shorts. White T-shirt. New shoes and socks. Songs downloaded. Earbuds in. Stretches—thighs, calves, hips, shoulders, arms.

Ready to run.

I take off down the driveway. Not quite the stride I imagined, but I'm off. I press PLAY and get into the rhythm. I bounce a bit and move my arms. Like the cross-country runners do.

I get to the end of our block. My calves start burning. Feel the burn. Yes. *Burn, baby, burn, calorie inferno*, I hear in my head. That's from Mom's *Dance Away the Pounds* retro workout DVD. I'm breathing. *Inhale, exhale.* I'm moving. I'm running. Like the wind. *Thud, thud, thud, thud.*

By the next corner, my breathing gets heavier. It's hot out. I start to sweat. My calves burn even more. Now my side starts hurting. I relax my pace. I must look like I'm in slow motion. But, hey, I'm doing it, right? I'm making an effort. I didn't get out of shape in a day—I'm not going to get healthy in a day.

Another block. I start wheezing. My calves and my thighs and my butt burn. I slow to a walk. Don't want to overdo on the first day.

I catch my breath and wipe my face with my hands. I think that'll do. I turn around and walk the three blocks back home. Tomorrow, it'll be four.

37

A FEW DAYS LATER, I COME DOWNSTAIRS IN MY running shoes. Mom notices, but says nothing. She hasn't said anything about anything—not about my exercising, my eating normal food like a normal person instead of a crazed lunatic, my initiative with Libby. Nothing. I bet she'd say something if I were sitting on the couch, pigging out.

I was so sure that once she saw that I was running, she'd horn in and want to train me. Weird thing is, I feel sort of disappointed that she didn't.

Judd zips around the table, and Gigi chases him. "Come on, Gigi, the aliens are getting away." He makes loud gurgling noises. Are they supposed to be the aliens or their spaceship? I'm afraid to ask.

Libby pouts at the table in front of a bowl of oatmeal.

"She's been sitting there for over an hour," Mom says when she sees me looking. "She keeps saying, 'No thank you, I couldn't eat another bite.'"

"Maybe she's not hungry."

"Oh, so you think you know, do you? How would *you* handle it?" Mom challenges me.

"I would let her choose not to eat but not let her snack on crap later. If she's really not hungry, then she'll be able to wait until lunch. If she's manipulating you, she'll learn that she can't."

"Okay," Mom moves to the table. "Let's try it." Then to Libby, "You know that if you don't eat breakfast, there's nothing else until lunch, right?"

"Right," says Libby.

"Go play."

Libby jumps down and chases Judd, pretending she's a wild alien.

Operation Healthy Libby is right on schedule. And Mom seems to be an ally.

I head out on my run. Or should I say almost run. I get a little bit farther than I did the last time, but not much. It's really muggy, and I start sweating within the first minute. This is not nearly as easy as it is in my imagination.

I decide to walk for a while. I start thinking about Raynee and Courtney and the Twisted Pretzel and if I want to go back to work there. I kind of do, but I can't believe how fast Mr. D. was willing to believe Courtney right off the bat. And I don't need the money as much, now that I quit S2S. But I could work with Raynee, and that's so much fun. I decide not to decide today.

Then I think about Naomi and all the crap she told me at the party. How much was true? Or was she in on Courtney's plan, trying to distract me? Is Dad really as bad as she said?

I also think about Cassie and what Raynee told me. How could I have been so clueless? Maybe it's hard to know until there's something else to compare it to.

Not to mention that photo thing. I didn't know the guy who posted it. Why would he take it down—especially since it had "likes"? Maybe I'll never know.

Before I know it, I'm standing outside Gram's garage. I key the code, knock twice, and yell, "Hey, Gram. It's me, Ann," as soon as I get inside.

"No need to yell. I'm right here." *Here* is perched on the couch, smoking and watching *Judge Judy*. "Oh, you're gonna get it now."

"Huh?"

"Not you. That fat ass on TV." Gram in sporting hot pink capris and a Hawaiian shirt.

"Oh, okay. What did she do?" I grab a glass from the kitchen and fill it with ice water and join her, careful to sit downwind.

"She lied, and it came back to bite her."

I chug about half of the water. I can't believe how hot it is today. Even stuffier at Gram's, since she keeps her house about eighty degrees all year long.

"Speaking of lying," I say, deciding to just come right out with it. "Did Dad really cheat on Mom with Nancy?"

The question seems to take Gram off guard. She stops mid-puff and coughs. "What the"—*cough*—"would make you"—*cough*—"ask about that?" *Cough, cough, cough.*

"Just wondering."

"Have you talked to your mom about it?" she says, catching her breath.

"No."

"Good. It'll only upset her. It wasn't easy, you know. Everything he put her through. Speaking of your mother, she says you quit that cockamamie diet you were on . . ."

Way to change the subject, Gram. "Yeah. I was tired of eating cardboard."

"Not to say I told you so, but—"

"I know. I know. Why? What did Mom say?" Just great! She doesn't say word one to me, but she tells Gram about it—how I failed at yet one more thing, no doubt. How I'm probably back to ice cream and Mega Mondo Combos for every meal.

"Nothing. Just that you weren't doing it anymore. That's all."

Yeah, right.

My turn to change the subject. "So what did my dad do to my mom?"

"I don't know what to tell you." She picks up the remote and turns down Judy reaming out some woman.

"Yeah, but I really want to know."

"Yes, well, he cheated on her, all right. Then lied to her about it. More than once, too. That fat ass Nancy wasn't the first. I'm surprised he hasn't cheated on *her.*"

"He may have."

Gram raises her eyebrows. "True. I wouldn't know if he did."

"Did he leave Mom for Nancy, or did Mom kick him out?"

"Your dad wouldn't ever have left." Gram puts out her cigarette and immediately lights another. "Why would he? He wanted to have his cake and eat it, too. Your mom couldn't live like that. And we agreed with her and supported her one hundred percent. But it wasn't easy, like I said. It was hard on her—raising two kids under five, pretty much on her own. Hard on all of you."

"Hard how?"

"It's always hard when you think someone who loves you doesn't think you're good enough," she says.

Tell me about it. I feel like that all the time. But somehow I feel like Gram is holding back. Not telling me everything. But she turns the volume up on the TV before I can ask.

"Jackie dropped off some invitations," she says, eyes on the screen. "Take them both, okay?" One white envelope is marked *Mr. and Mrs. Michael Logan and family*. Another says *Ann Galardi*. I get my own invitation—like an adult, not an add-on to the Logan family?

I open it. The inside envelope says *Ann + 1*. There's also another card and envelope. "What's all this extra stuff? And what does *plus one* mean?"

Gram holds up her finger. Judge Judy is laying down her verdict. I look over the invitation while I wait. The letters are raised—fancy. It's weird seeing *Jacqueline Marie Curtis and Christine Elizabeth Pierce* instead of *Jackie and Chris*. It doesn't mention the ceremony in the park, only announces the wedding and gives the time of the reception and the address of the reception hall.

After the credits roll, Gram tells me that *plus one* means I get to invite a guest. Really? Like a date? I've never heard of that before. If only I had someone to invite. Jon finally accepted my friend request, but that's a long way from a date. It's even a long way from another conversation!

She explains how to fill out the RSVP card and then says that the actual ceremony is going to be very intimate—about thirty-five to forty people. The invitations are for the reception, where there will be more guests.

While I'm looking over everything, Gram says, "Oh, and I talked to Tony today."

No freaking way! For real? My face must've said what my voice couldn't, because she says, "He just called out of the blue."

"What did he say?" I sit at the table, ready to hear all the details.

"He finished his first year at Grand Valley, 3.8 GPA. He's working two jobs—waiting tables at Olive Garden and loading trucks at UPS. He's got a girlfriend named Allie. She's from Ohio. Oh, and he might come to the wedding."

"Really?" I actually bounce up and down in my seat like a five-year-old.

"He got your message on Facebook and called to ask if I thought he should come."

"And you said yes, of course."

"Not exactly." Gram grabs her cigarettes and sits at the table with me.

"What do you mean *not exactly*?"

"I told him that I'd love to see him." She lights up and takes a drag. "But that this is Jackie and Chris's day and not the time to rehash things, start drama, or draw attention away from them in any way. And that includes upsetting your mother."

"Do you think he would do that?" My stomach knots just remembering the way things were before he left. I want my brother back—the one who protected me, told funny stories, and made everyone laugh. I don't want the button-pushing instigator.

"I would hope not," she says, "but I needed to make sure he understands."

"Do you think he'll come? And why didn't he e-mail *me*?"

"Couldn't tell you, on either count." Gram flicks ashes in her ashtray. "You'll have to ask him, but I wouldn't hold your breath. I'll be surprised if he shows up."

When I think of the havoc Tony's capable of wreaking, I don't know if I want him to come after all.

38

WHEN I GET HOME, MOM IS ON THE PHONE IN
the laundry room and the twins are glued to a blaring TV, eating caramel corn out of the box by the handful. Gigi lies between
them, snaffling up stray pieces.

What the hell? I thought Mom wasn't going to give Libby garbage! They probably swiped it while she wasn't paying attention.

I pick up the box. "Come on, you guys. It's almost time for lunch.
All this sugar isn't good for you."

"Does it make you fat?" asks Libby.

"It makes *you* fat." Judd pushes Libby's belly.

"Justice Michael!" I yell. "Don't ever do that again. Libby is *not*
fat. And it's not about fat, it's about what is good for your body,
Liberty." Now I sound like Mom. Lord, help me. Being a bystander
is way easier.

"You're not the boss of me." Judd grabs the caramel corn out of
my hand.

I grab it back and roll up the foil bag inside the box. "After
lunch," I say. "Maybe."

"Mom!" Judd bangs on the laundry room door. "Ann took our caramel corn!"

"Yeah," Libby joins in, reaching for the box. "Mommy! We want our caramel corn back."

"No." I hold the box over my head. "Mom said no snacks. Libby didn't eat her breakfast."

The twins keep yelling, which makes Gigi bark. I can't tell if she's on my side or theirs, but I'm pretty sure by the way she's dancing on her hind legs that she wants the twins to win.

Mom storms out of the laundry room with the phone to her ear and a psychotic look on her face. It's her can't-you-see-I'm-on-the-phone-shut-up-now look. And it's directed at me. Only me. She reaches up, snatches the box that I'm holding above my head, and hands it to the twins. Judd smirks in satisfaction, and the two of them return to the blaring TV.

Mom says, "Just a second, okay?" Then she covers the phone with her hand and hisses through clenched teeth, "Really, Ann! Stealing snacks from the kids! Please! I need to take this call!" Then she shoots me another look before she slams the door behind her.

This is bullshit. Absolute bullshit. She thinks I took the caramel corn from the twins *for myself*. She's so oblivious that she probably doesn't even remember our conversation earlier. If I thought she could be an ally in Operation Libby, I was wrong. Apparently, I'm on my own.

39

I CHECK FACEBOOK. CASSIE'S STATUS IS *MISSING Maddy.* ☹ Then I see that she's written on my wall: *Haven't seen you in forever. Let's hang out.* No thanks.

Raynee texts me after lunch, and we meet at the mall. I'm glad, because I can't take being in the house one more minute. That alone is reason to keep working at the Twisted Pretzel. I pick her up from her shift, and as soon as Mr. D. sees me, he apologizes for jumping to conclusions. And for not calling days ago. That he's meant to, but he's been busy covering shifts in Jackson and managing the other stores. He asks if he can put me back on the schedule. I apologize for walking out and tell him I'd love that. All is right with my employment. The Twisted Pretzel is the least twisted part of my life.

Once Raynee gets off work, she says she's starving—she refused to eat one thing while she was working now that she knows they keep such close tabs—so the first place we go is Applebee's. I already ate, but I order a Diet Coke and wind up eating a few of the celery sticks that come with her Buffalo chicken strips.

We talk about our families and how Raynee's parents are divorced, too, only kind of recently, so she's still upset about it. We talk about that for a long time.

And about the party. Apparently Courtney let Naomi spike her own drinks, too, to keep me from getting suspicious—but Naomi had no idea what was really going on. Plus, turns out she's known for getting drunk and spilling her guts (which Raynee thought I knew). Only Courtney, Tiffany, and Melanie were trying to make me look bad. Even though Naomi and I have nothing in common except my father, and we've never been close, I'm relieved that she wasn't in on it.

And about Jon. (Jon *Reilly*, I remind myself.) I tell her about buying the running shoes. And she tells me that Jon had asked *both* Raynee and Courtney about me—my name, and where I went to school. She didn't think much about it. But Courtney's been pushing Jon to date Tiffany, and Courtney probably thinks I messed that up. I don't know how, though. It's not like we're together.

About Jared, and how he cheated on her, but she kept taking him back. She says that she's hoping that she finally has the courage to walk away. I hope so, too. She's too good for him, and I tell her that.

Then about Aunt Jackie's wedding and how I need to find a dress. "They gave me my own invitation with a plus one." I say.

"So you can invite someone. . . . How about Jon?"

"I don't think so." I tie a knot in a straw wrapper. "The last time I saw him, I puked on him. Kind of hard to go from there to my aunt's wedding, you know?"

She laughs. "I guess you're right."

The waitress brings the check.

"Hey, Raynee, why don't *you* be my plus one?"

"Really?" She seems surprised. And happy.

I smile. "Yes, really."

"Let's get out of here." Raynee lays out dollar bills from her tips to pay the check and scoots out of the booth. "We need to find you a bridesmaid's dress."

Oh, no. I didn't tell her about the dress because I wanted her to go shopping with me. I have a hard enough time as it is; I do not need more witnesses. I certainly don't want to advertise the fact that I don't fit into anything at the cool stores like Snapz!, and I would never, never, *never* ask Raynee—a Knee, former or not—to shop in the fat stores.

I follow anyway. Maybe I can fake it, or distract her. I stop at Payless. "Why don't we look for shoes instead?"

Raynee keeps walking. "Not until we find a dress, silly." Then she suggests Keehn's. I try telling her that Mom and I already went there, but she claims that she is skilled beyond imagination in finding dresses.

Before we get there, though, I yank her into the nearest store. "What did you do that for?"

"Look." I point from behind a jeans display. Jon. He walks by with a couple of his friends. I'm terrified to see him again, after what I did to him. Nobody wants to be puked on.

"Ooh, let's follow them and say hi."

"No way! So he can tell everyone that I'm *that* girl and see them all get grossed out?" I gross out enough people just being me. I don't need them picturing me hurling.

"True." She pulls a few dresses of a nearby rack. "So what about these?"

It is then that I realize that the store I yanked Raynee into is Snapz! How can I get her out of here and still maintain a shred of dignity?

She runs to the back—to the clearance prom dresses—and squeals. "Ann, come here. Look."

I suck in a deep breath, hold it, and walk back there, desperate to think of some reason that I can't try any of them on. *I'm morally opposed to taffeta? I'm allergic to the color green? Sequins scare me? I feel like I'm going to throw up.* (That one came to me thanks to Jon.)

Raynee holds up a really cute salmon strapless with a full skirt, Snapz! size three. "And it's only thirty dollars after you take an additional fifty percent off the clearance price. They're practically giving it away."

I can't argue with that. It's cute and it's cheap. But it's too small.

She holds it up to me. "The color is gorgeous with your skin tone, hair, and eyes. Gorgeous! You've got to try it on."

"Um," I stammer. "I don't know."

"Come on! What do you have to lose?" She nods to a clerk to open a dressing room.

About thirty-one more pounds. My dignity. My self-respect, what's left of it. And—thinking back to the the last time I tried on a Snapz! dress—my life. Those things are dangerous.

"I don't know." I hesitate and inspect it for a flaw. Anything. "Maybe we should keep looking. Maybe there's something at Keehn's."

"You don't like it, do you?" She holds the dressing room door open.

I give her a not-really look. Maybe that'll work. I cannot. Under any circumstances. Get in that dressing room.

"They never look good on the hanger," she says. "Try it anyway."

Just as I'm about to object, from the corner of my eye, I see Jon and his friends coming into the store. One guy picks up a shirt from the display and throws it at another guy. I can't let Jon see me.

I grab the dress, step into the dressing room, and close and lock the door behind me. I'll fake it. I'll pretend to try it on. I'll say it's not cut right. That's what Mom always says. That must be why it's on clearance, I'll say. It'll work. Then, when Jon and his friends are long gone, I'll escape.

"Raynee?" Jon's voice, close by. "Hey."

I back up against the wall, so my feet aren't visible, and stand perfectly still. Frozen. Hoping Raynee doesn't tell him I'm in there. *Please, Raynee. Please.*

"Hey, Jon. Shop Snapz! often?"

He laughs. "Mason's getting his sister a gift card for her birthday."

It's quiet. What's going on? Did he leave? Can I come out? *Someone say something.*

"Great party last week," Jon says finally.

"Thanks."

"Yeah, uh, well, I've been meaning to call you."

I knew it. Jon must like Raynee. Not me.

"Yeah?"

"Yeah. How well do you know that Ann girl?"

Ann? That's *me*! Oh God.

"Pretty well," says Raynee with a slight giggle. "She's great."

206

Thanks, Raynee.

"Yeah. How's she doing after the party? She was pretty sick."

I cringe.

"No thanks to your cousin. Court spiked her drinks without telling her."

"She is such a bitch sometimes," he says. There's another pause. I'm guessing Raynee is nodding. I know I am.

Then out of nowhere, Jon says, "Do you think Ann would mind if I called her?"

Holy shit! Did he just say what I think he did? Call me? *Me?* My stomach quavers, and my heart is thumping like I did two high-intensity workouts back-to-back. It's not cold in the dressing room, but I'm shaking.

The last time a boy—Tyler Biggs—called me was to ask to borrow my science notes because he'd been sick with mono. After I said he could, he hung up without saying thanks or good-bye.

"I think she'd be fine with you calling her." Raynee's voice is affected, louder, as if she wants to make sure I heard her. "Give me your phone and I'll put her number in it."

Silence. Again. Can they hear my heart pounding?

"Cool," he finally says. "Thanks."

"Okay, dude, got it. Let's go." I'm guessing that was Mason.

And then he's gone. I exhale and realize that I'd been holding my breath.

40

"LET ME IN." RAYNEE KNOCKS ON THE DRESSING room door.

I rip the dress off the hanger and unzip it as I unlock the door. "It doesn't fit," I say as she bursts in.

"Did you hear what he said?" Raynee squeals. "He wants to call you!"

"Yes." I fight back a big, cheesy, stupid grin, but my face dimples, according to the full-length mirror, so I give in and smile. I can't help it.

"What about the dress? What did you think?"

I grimace.

"Let me see," she insists. "Put it back on."

I stand there looking like an idiot. I can't tell her. It's the biggest size in the store. *Tell her. She'll understand.* But what if she doesn't? What if she's disgusted? What if it's the end of our friendship? *Tell her. Open up to someone. Come on, take a chance.*

I take a deep breath and let it go. "It doesn't fit."

"That doesn't matter," she says.

"*Doesn't matter?* Of course it matters."

"No, it doesn't. Put it on." She's getting louder. I don't want to make a scene.

Keeping my clothes on, I step into the dress and pull it up over my boobs. Then I slip my shirt out from under it, so I don't have to get undressed in front of Raynee. I'm mortified by how much skin shows across my shoulders. The dress is gorgeous, though; she's right about that. But I can tell already that it won't zip all the way.

Raynee stands behind me and tugs at the zipper. It moves up more than halfway, which is farther than I thought it would.

"Don't break it," I whisper.

"Hmmm," she says. "Wait here. Don't move. I have an idea."

"Raynee . . ." I begin, but she's gone before I can protest.

In no time she's back with three long, sheer, white scarves.

"What are these?" I ask.

"Scarves. Duh."

"I know that, but why?"

"Just humor me a second, will you?" She stuffs the ends of two of the scarves into the front of the dress. "Hold these." Then she drapes them over each shoulder and spins me around to look in the mirror. "See? I can sew these into the front here, pull them to the back, and sew them across here." Her fingers slide across the back of the dress. "And then let the rest of the scarf flow off the back. So elegant, don't you think?"

I nod, in spite of myself. It really looks pretty. "But it won't zip."

"That's what this other scarf is for." She folds it several times.

"See?" I clearly don't, so she runs her finger along the bodice under my armpits. "I'll rip out this seam on each side and stitch in a tiny panel that matches the straps. Once the scarf is folded a couple of times, it's not sheer anymore. By the time I'm done with it, it'll look custom-made.

"And the scarves are only"—she grabs the price tag—"five bucks each! Clearance, baby! You can get the whole thing for about forty-five bucks! You can't even buy *materials* for that."

I don't know what to say. I knew Raynee sewed, but it never occurred to me that she was a miracle worker.

"Come on, don't look so surprised. You knew I altered my clothes."

"Altered, you know, a nip here, a tuck there. Not total revamp."

She laughs. "Everyone in my family sews. Mom says we Gilbert women have to because of how we're built."

I'm confused. "How you're built?"

"Yeah. Come on. Don't tell me you haven't noticed how out of proportion I am."

"I haven't." And that's the truth. Raynee's so cute and has the tiniest waist. I can't imagine what she's talking about.

"All of us—my grandma, mom, aunts, sisters—are pear-shaped. Same wide-load hips, little waist and tiny chest. Nana says our family tree is a pear tree. Try finding a dress *that* out of proportion. We have to alter everything."

"Wow" is all I can say. I'm amazed. It never occurred to me to change *the clothes* to fit *me*. I always thought it had to be the other way around. And it never occurred to me that people who aren't overweight could have trouble with off-the-rack sizes.

"That's why it doesn't matter if the dress fits. It only matters if you like it. So? Do you?" She's so excited.

I look in the mirror. At me in a Snapz! size three dress. A beautiful salmon dress—the color I wanted—with a full skirt. I twirl like Libby playing dress-up. "I do now."

41

I CONSIDER CALLING MOM BEFORE I BUY IT TO SEE what she thinks, but I change my mind when I remember the swimsuit fiasco. She'll just talk me out of it. It doesn't zip, and she doesn't know Raynee or her freaking amazing sewing skills. And she has her heart set on a tight, slinky thing. Which is great for her, but Aunt Jackie already said I could wear what I wanted, and this is what I want.

Mom is stunned speechless when I get home. Not only do I have a new friend, and not only is she a seamstress, but I also found a dress for the wedding. And, to top it off, Mom loves it.

The whole time I was telling the story and Raynee was showing her the alteration plan, Mom never said a word. She just stood there, listening, her head tilted like Gigi. By the time we were finished, though, she was practically giddy.

In fact, Mom drags us back to Snapz! immediately and finds the same dress in her size. No altering required. But when Raynee says that she can take in the skirt to be tighter, Mom decides to get it altered anyway.

"That way," Raynee tells us after Mom models her dress for us, "we can use the fabric from the skirt for Ann's panels." Then she drapes one of the scarves around Mom's neck and lets it hang down her back. Her skin is still exposed, and she matches me. "So now there's a scarf left for you."

"Perfect." Mom stands in front of the full-length mirror in her bedroom. "It's like having our own fashion designer. Thank you!"

"No problem." Raynee smiles. So do I.

Mom keeps shooting me looks when Raynee isn't looking. I know she's happy I have a friend—and that she likes her—but God, I wish she'd stop it.

"Raynee's going to be my plus one for the wedding," I say. "That's okay, right?"

"Of course!" Mom says. "Good idea."

"Mommy! Mommy! Mommy!" Libby and Judd rush into Mom's room.

"They have new toys at Mondo Burger." Libby jumps up and down like Santa just called and said he's on his way.

"The TV said so," says Judd.

"We want Smiley Meals," says Libby.

"Can we, can we, pleeease?" Judd plasters on his best smile.

"Please." Libby poses with her face pressed up against his, like they're ready for the photographer. Or an Academy Award.

Raynee laughs. "They're so cute!"

Mom smiles. "If you're good while Mommy gets some work done, we'll see."

We'll see is code. For the twins it means "yes, probably, unless something major happens." For me it means "not likely, unless something major happens." Mom always leaves room for that major development or the right to change her mind. The kids know this, too, so they run out of the room screaming and cheering. They vow to be good.

"Oh, Ann," says Mom. "I've been meaning to ask you. Is there any way you can help me with the kids next week? Donna's going on vacation."

"Um . . ." How can I get out of this? "I probably have to work."

"I'd only *need* you in the morning. Please." She begs like the twins coercing for Smiley Meals. "I can go to work to take care of the important stuff and be back around one-ish."

"We'll see," I say. Raynee catches my eye and winks.

After we go downstairs, she tells me that she can cover for me at work if I want to babysit. She didn't want to say anything in front of Mom, in case I was trying to get out of it. How she is just so instinctively cool is beyond me.

After she leaves, I go for my run—six blocks this time!—and then to Mondo Burger with the fam. I have mixed feelings, but Operation Healthy Libby is still on track, and I need to be there to make it happen.

The twins sing the Mondo Burger theme song all the way there. You'd think we were headed to Disney World or something. Mike and Mom talk about their days—work, our dresses for the wedding, cute things the twins say.

I think about Jon. *Will he really call? When?* I check my phone. Charge, yes. Service, three bars. Missed call, no.

Mondo Burger is packed. We wait in line forever. Mike lets the twins order their own. Smiley Meals, of course. I order a Mondo salad with chicken. Mom orders the same, with a smile at me— the Suzy Galardi-Logan Seal of Approval. I want to tell her that

I'm doing it for Libby, not for her, but I don't. Mike orders a Mega Mondo Combo and a Coke. A twinge of jealousy ripples through my gut. I'd love a Mega Mondo burger. And then a twinge of despair. Will I ever get to eat burgers again? Without guilt? Without gaining?

I know the answer, and I don't like it. Although maybe a Junior Mondo will work. One day.

The kids and I claim a table and wait for Mike to pay and bring over the tray. Mom grabs napkins and ketchup in little white paper cups. I won't need ketchup. I love ketchup.

The twins flatten out their burger wrappers like plates and arrange their burgers, fries, and ketchup on them. Mike takes a big bite. "Mmmm."

"I don't know how you can eat that stuff." Mom squeezes about a third of her dressing packet onto her salad and mixes it with her fork. "If I ate that I'd be as big as . . ."

At first I think she's going to say "Ann," but she doesn't. I pour on a whole packet of dressing. It's fat-free, and there's no way I could eat salad without it.

". . . as big as that woman over there. I bet she eats here every day."

A large couple is packed into a booth on the other side of the dining area. I want to block them from Mom's view and comments. I want to stand up and put a tarp around them, protect them. So what if they eat here every day? So what? Are they hurting anyone? And maybe they don't eat here that much. Maybe they've been on diet after diet and are tired of eating salads and are eating the first burger they've had all year. Who knows? I don't, and neither does Mom. She doesn't know anything. She has no idea what it feels like to have to make choices every meal between what you want to eat and what you should eat. She *likes* this stuff.

Libby must've heard her, too, because she stops eating and looks over at the woman. She sits back in her chair and says, "I'm full. I couldn't possibly eat another bite."

"You hardly touched your burger, honey," says Mike. "Why don't you have a little more?"

Mom turns back to her. "Eat your dinner, Libby. You've wanted your Smiley Meal all day. Here it is. Eat it."

"I'm full," she repeats.

Judd is oblivious. He makes motor sounds as he flies his toy across his food and all around. Then he takes a bite and starts all over again. He is in Mondo Burger heaven.

"Want some of my salad, Lib?" I take a bite to show her how appetizing it is. "It's good."

"No." She sits back and crosses her arms in front of her.

Mom picks up a fry, dips it in ketchup, and holds it out to Libby, making it dance. "Come on, honey, eat it."

I take one and eat it. "Mmm. They're yummy. If you don't eat them, I will."

"Go ahead," says Libby.

Somehow I have a feeling that my eating a fry doesn't affect Libby because I'm fat. But Mom . . . if Mom eats one, that might be different. "Here, Mom, try one. They're really good."

"I'm sure they are, but they're Libby's. I don't want to eat her dinner."

Come on, Mom, show her. Show her that it's okay to eat something. Just one.

216

"Libby won't care, will you, Lib?" I refuse to give up. "Come on, Mom, try one."

"I need more ketchup," says Judd.

Mom jumps up like she's on fire. "I'll get it."

Then it hits me. Mom *cannot* eat a fry. I try to remember the last time I actually saw her have fries or ice cream or anything remotely unhealthy. I can't. I never see her eat junk. She buys it and feeds it to us—but she never eats it herself. What is she afraid of? If it were just about health, she wouldn't buy it for us, right? Is she that afraid of getting fat? Or of looking like that woman across the room?

Of looking like me?

42

THE NEXT MONDAY I WEIGH MYSELF. DOWN THREE and half more pounds. Almost twenty gone—twenty-seven and a half left to go. The closest I've ever gotten to this is the first time I was on Weight Watchers. I lost seventeen pounds and earned a keychain. I found it all again, and then some, in less than a year.

Why does it have to be so hard? This time, when I lose the weight, I'll never put it on again. I've fought too hard to get here. Still, I'm also battling another thought: Once I'm thin and can have cheeseburgers and candy bars in moderation, will I be able to stop myself? Will I end up back here again, like I have in the past? Or will I have to be like Mom, denying myself everything? I don't want to think about that. Not today, anyway. Today I'm on my way toward being thinner. Healthier. Happier.

I help Mom with the kids, not because I want to help her, but because I want to help Libby. All this week I babysit until one or so, go for a run, and then work until close. I'm tired and want to lie on the couch and watch TV. But that is not the example I want to set.

"Let's practice the Thriller." Libby runs to Mom's iPod dock.

I'd rather fight real zombies than hear that song ever again. But Libby has it playing before I can object. It triggers Fourth of July party memories. Of Courtney. Of spinning and hurling. Of embarrassment. Of Jon, who still hasn't called.

Judd gets fired up and bounces all over the place. Libby poses and gets ready. Once she starts dancing, I'm surprised how good she is. She must have really paid attention in those classes. She has those steps down.

"Dance with me," she says.

She's so cute I can't resist. We step and move and groove for nearly an hour. Libby presses the repeat button without asking if I want to. It never ceases to amaze me how four-year-olds never get bored watching the same show or movie or doing the same thing over and over and over. It uses up a lot of the morning, and since it's exercise, I don't feel guilty about skipping the workout DVD.

When it's time for lunch, I make vegetable soup and cheese sandwiches without asking them what they want. If I ask, they'll each want something different, and there is no easy way to convince them to give in to each other. And I don't want to make two things or deal with attitude. Besides, if I'm going to model health, I want to make something kind of healthy, but still something they'll eat.

I get a text from Cassie. *Sat. night. Me & U. Movie!*

I text back. *Sorry. I have plans.*

And I do. Raynee and I already have a date to give each other manis and pedis. She's been after me to teach her the Thriller. I'd told her no, absolutely not, not even if Hell froze over. But after this morning, I decide to do it. If anyone had told me six months ago that *I'd* be teaching *Raynee Gilbert* how to dance, and that I'd brush off Cassie to do it, I'd have called them a liar.

The Devil had better buy himself a snow blower because the climate is changing.

"You guys are really good dancers." I sit down and eat with the kids and crumble a few crackers in my soup. Libby watches and crushes some in hers, too, and then so does Judd. I don't talk about the food at all. I don't talk about fat. I just talk about other stuff. And I eat. Like it's no big deal. Just something we do. Not a big production. Every day this week, we eat like normal people—breakfast and lunch, with no fights, power struggles, or problems.

Dinner is another matter. Mom is there for dinner.

I start paying attention to how often Mom mentions words like *fat*, *too much food*, or *diet*. I'm surprised. In one meal alone I count thirteen *fats*, which also includes two *fattenings* and one *fatter*.

I also start really watching how much Mom eats compared to how much she talks about eating. If someone only listened to what she says, they'd think she ate a lot and all the time. She doesn't. She puts tiny amounts on her plate, but only eats about a third to a half of it. She pushes it around and jumps up from the table, waiting on everyone. She grabs more napkins and condiments, refills drinks, and answers the phone. I guess I've spent so much time avoiding her glares and comments that I never noticed *her* habits.

Libby hasn't missed a thing. No wonder she has such a messed up idea about food. I model overeating, and Mom models eating disorders. Was she always like this? I've always thought Mom doesn't get it. Get *me*. But maybe I don't get *her*, either. Does she even know how she comes off, *why* she's like this? Libby needs normal, something in the middle. Between Mom and me. Not obsessed with food, but not obsessed with weight either. Moderation. Focusing on that—and Libby, instead of me, me, me all the time—feels good. Like that's how it should be.

august

43

TWO WEEKS AND FOUR AND HALF POUNDS LATER,
I decide to purge all traces of the fatter me. The first to go is the
S2S diet crap. Except the exercise bands and DVD—I like them.
Trashing those boxes is the most satisfying part of the whole program, although part of me feels guilty for wasting food, especially
since it was so expensive. But I'm never going to eat it. Just the
thought of the lasagna makes me shudder.

After that, I grab another large garbage bag and head to my
room. I never wanted to clean up my clothes before, because I
didn't want to get rid of anything I hoped would fit someday. But
now a lot of it's too *big*! I fill two large garbage bags in no time, and
I can see the floor for the first time in I don't know how long.

Then I excavate a treasure. At the very bottom of a huge pile in
my closet, I find my copy of *Slimmer You*—tattered, dog-eared, and
held together with strips of purple duct tape. The bottom right
corner of the cover is ripped—a casualty of Gigi's puppyhood.

I flip through the pages and laugh at side notes from my
younger self: *Yeah, right!* (on the page about leaving food on your

plate), *Ann and Cassie, BFFs forever!!!* on the back, and *I hate her!*, which was probably about Mom.

Then I find an old pic tucked inside. Mom, Tony, Gram, and I are standing on Gram's porch. I remember this! It was the summer before fourth grade, and I thought I was enormous. I put it in *Slimmer You* as my *before* shot. Now that I look at it, though, I wasn't really that big. A little pudgy, sure. But not fat.

Then I see Mom. Oh my God! She's so thin. Her arm is about half the size of mine, even though I'm a kid. No wonder I thought I was fat. Compared to her, I was.

I slip the picture back and tuck *Slimmer You* into my nightstand. Even though I have it practically memorized and it's in rough shape, I'm not getting rid of it. It's more than a weight loss guide; it's my childhood diary.

Once I pull out everything that doesn't fit, I'm surprised how empty my closet is. I need to go shopping, so I text Raynee. We decide to go to Keehn's before work.

~~~~~

"About time you got some new clothes," she says as we meet up in the juniors' section.

"Do I look that bad?" I stand in front of a mirrored post.

"Not bad. Just . . . baggy." She pulls the back of my shirt so it's tighter on the sides. "See? You need something that really fits."

All the summer clothes are on clearance, so we start there. I grab a couple of pairs of shorts and some cute shirts. The brown bathing suit with the stripes is marked down, half off. I take that, too.

"Has Jon called yet?" Raynee asks.

"Not yet." I move to a rack of dressier clothes and pick up a few more things. "But his Facebook status earlier in the week said he was in Florida."

"That would explain why I haven't seen him around the mall lately."

"I guess."

"I'll talk to Melanie," she says. "Maybe she'll know what's going on with him."

He's probably partying in Florida, not giving me a second thought. "I'll be right back." I hold up the hangers. "I'm going to try these on."

"Okay." I'm glad she doesn't follow me. I'm still really self-conscious about trying on clothes, especially now that I have no idea how to gauge what'll fit.

I start with the swimsuit. I slip the bottoms on over my under-wear. They're loose. Too loose. I try on the top, and it is, too. And, so is everything else. I shimmy and let a pair of buttoned shorts drop to the ground. Then I throw everything back on hangers and hurry back for smaller sizes.

"How did it go?" Raynee's holding a pair of jean shorts and a couple of tanks.

"Still trying." I search the rack for the suit in size 15. There isn't one. But there is a 13. It can't hurt to try, can it? I remember the killer rubber band at Snapz! and put it back.

"Oh, that's so cute!" Raynee hands it to me. "Take it."

I do and head back to the dressing room. The size 15 shorts fit pretty well. A flouncy shirt—size extra-large—looks really cute with it. I pop my head out of the dressing rooms and wave Raynee in. "What do you think?"

"I like the shorts, but the shirt's still too big." She wrinkles her nose. "What size is it?"

I hesitate a moment, but then I tell her.

"Let me get another one. Be right back."

"Here." She tosses a large over the door. "Try this."

I put it on. It's tighter and shorter than I'm used to. "I don't know."

"Let me see," she says. I open the door. "Ann, it's really cute. That's how it's supposed to fit. You need to get it. And wear it."

"You think so?"

"I know so." She grabs the extra-large. "I'll hang it up. Now try on that suit. I'll be right back."

I look at the suit. I can't wear a size 13. Can I? If I don't at least try before Raynee gets back, I'll have to undress in front of her. I tug it on. It's snug, but not tight.

"Well?" Raynee's back. I unlock the door. She peeks in. "Love it! Buy it! We'll hang out by my pool after work."

I look in the mirror and suck in my gut. "You don't think it's too small?"

"Ann! It's a swimsuit, not a tunic."

I buy it, along with the shorts, shirt, and an outfit for the rehearsal dinner—a stretchy-waist skirt, a button-down top, and a tank for underneath—all on clearance.

Then we move to the shoe department to find shoes for the wedding. We find some cute strappy heels that will match my dress perfectly.

I hobble around a display. "How will I walk in these all day?" I don't have much experience with anything higher than pumps.

"Wear them around the house and practice," says Raynee. "It's really not that hard."

Since the only other options are closed-toed pumps or flat sandals, I go with the heels.

On the way through the mall to the Twisted Pretzel, Raynee asks, "How much have you lost anyway?"

"About twenty pounds." Actually, it's twenty-two.

"Wow!" she says. "Have you tried on the dress lately?" I shake my head. It hadn't occurred to me. "Because I bet I'll have to remove the panels before the wedding!"

I catch a full-length glimpse of myself in a store mirror. Could Raynee be right? Could I really be a Snapz! size three? Just the thought of it makes me practically bubbly.

44

BY THE TIME AUNT JACKIE AND CHRIS'S REHEARSAL dinner rolls around I've lost another five and a half pounds—twenty-seven and a half altogether!—and Raynee does have to pull the panels from my dress. I tell her I'm sorry that she has to redo her custom work, but she says she's glad to do it. I still have seventeen and a half pounds to go before I hit my goal, which is still two pounds more than the high end on the ideal weight chart for my height, but I'm feeling pretty okay. Better than okay. I've lost more weight than I ever have before. And I'm wearing a Snapz! dress—a legit size three, since only the straps are customized—to the wedding!

Jon still hasn't called. His most current Facebook status from four days ago is: *I'm home.* Sometimes I think I imagined him asking for my number. Raynee insists that I didn't, but I'm not convinced. Is there such a thing as a dual delusion?

At the rehearsal, pretty much everyone tells me that I look good. The only person who mentions weight, though, is Tayla. "Your face is so much thinner, I hardly recognized you." I assume it's a compliment, but I'm not sure what to say. I just smile.

The dinner is in the small banquet room of a fancy restaurant. We can have anything we want. Aunt Jackie and Chris have been living together for years and are pretty established in their careers, so they've insisted on paying for everything themselves.

I order from their "light side" menu—pasta with grilled chicken, broccoli, mushrooms, tomatoes, and onions topped with a light tomato garlic sauce. It's really good. Mike orders a steak, and Mom gets—surprise, surprise—a salad, dressing on the side. The twins have mac and cheese.

Gram orders fettuccini alfredo. "Who cares if I eat like a fat ass," she announces. "When you get to be my age, nobody's looking anyway."

That's all it takes. "I'm full," says Libby. "I couldn't eat another bite."

"Come on, honey," Mom coos. "Eat up your macaroni, and you can have ice cream."

Libby's eyes light up. She loves ice cream, and being four, she hasn't figured out what's fattening and what isn't.

"I want ice cream now," she says. "I don't want any more fat ass macaroni."

At that, the whole table erupts in laughter. I'm not sure what's funny about a little kid swearing, but it is. Mike corrects her, though. He has to. He's the dad.

"I want ice cream, too," says Judd.

"Only if Libby eats all her macaroni," says Mom.

"Eat, Libby, eat," Judd chants. "Eat, Libby, eat."

"I said," Libby announces, "I don't want any more. I couldn't eat another bite."

"If you're full, you don't have room for ice cream," says Mom.

"Yes, I do," says Libby. "Ice cream will melt down and around all the macaroni in my tummy. It doesn't need any room." More laughter.

"She's got you there, Mom," I say.

"Don't encourage her." Mom decides to hold her ground. "No ice cream, unless you eat your macaroni."

Judd scarfs down his and then tries to coax Libby to eat hers. She's stubborn and refuses. Besides, history has taught her that she'll get ice cream anyway.

Then dessert is served. I wait for Mom to take Libby's ice cream away, but she doesn't. She lets her dig right in.

Then the waitress serves Mom. She says, "None for me, thanks. *I'm* watching my waistline, and ice cream is way too fattening the day before a wedding." She directs her comment to everyone eating ice cream and smiles at the waitress like her self-control is going to win her a medal.

I see Libby deflate, as if she's thinking, *Not* ice cream, *too.*

I can't take it anymore. I'm sick of every single word out of Mom's mouth having to do with weight. Who cares if she eats ice cream or not? If she doesn't want any, why can't she just refuse it and shut up? What's the big deal if some people want some? Why can't she let people eat without guilt?

"Why do you have to always do that?" I say.

"Do what?" asks Mom.

"Make anyone who eats feel guilty."

"I don't."

"Yes, you do. Every time I put food in my mouth, you glare at me. And you've got Libby a nervous wreck that she's going to get fat."

By now, all the isolated pods of conversation have quieted and everyone is listening to us. I'm making a scene. *Stop. Shut up. Leave it alone.*

"What's a nervous wreck?" Judd asks Libby.

"It means when you have an accident 'cause you're scared. I didn't pee, though, Annie. I don't even gotta go."

Everyone laughs at that, and it breaks the mood a little. Good. Maybe they'll go back to talking and forget I said anything.

Except Mom doesn't let it drop. She's not laughing at all. It's like she doesn't hear Libby or Judd. "You don't know what you're talking about. Libby is fine."

"Is she?" I glare at her.

"Yes, I am fine, Annie. You can't get fat if you don't each much food. Right, Mommy?"

The room falls dead silent.

Mom looks shocked. Good. Finally.

"See?" I practically scream. "You're making her anorexic. And she's *four*!" I get up. I have to leave. I. Am. Making. A. Scene. But before I get through the door, I yell, "Being fat isn't the worst thing that can happen to a person. Look, I'm still kicking." I fling my arms up like a demented game show model. "It's way worse just being Suzanne Galardi-Logan's kid!"

I hear a gasp but do not look around. I can't. Instead, I run to the bathroom, lock myself in a stall, and bawl. I hate her. I hate what she's done to me, and what's she's doing to Libby. And she's totally clueless. She's so obsessed with having everything so picture perfect that she's screwed up everything.

Within a few minutes, Gram comes in the bathroom. "Come on, Ann," she says. "You're coming home with me tonight. We'll stop at the house so you can get your dress and stuff to get ready for the wedding."

Leave it to Gram to fix everything. Like always.

45

THE NEXT MORNING, GRAM HAS HER COFFEE AND
a couple of cigarettes. Then she volunteers to do my hair for the
wedding. I'm skeptical because, while I love Gram dearly, her style
doesn't exactly match mine—or anyone else's, for that matter. She
drags out a couple of curling irons, hot rollers, hair spray, combs,
clips, and even glitter spray—where did she get *that*?—and sets
up shop at the kitchen table. She's pretty insistent that she knows
just how to do it, so I relent, but I'm afraid. Very afraid.

First, she combs out my hair and sprays it down. Then she rolls
up a chunk of hair onto the biggest roller. When she puts the pin
to hold it in I think my scalp is frying. "It's hot."

She adjusts it. "Is this better?"

"Yes."

While she rolls up the next one, she says, "You owe your mother
an apology. Jackie and Chris, too."

What? Where did this come from? I thought she was on *my*
side.

"You were way out of line treating your mother like that. In front of everyone." She reaches behind her with a chunk of my hair still in her hand and grabs her cigarettes, taps the green and white pack, pops it in her mouth, leans in, and lights it. I worry that she's going to ignite my hair, too. I squirm, sweat rising to the surface of my scalp and neck. And not just because she's smoking a couple of inches from my hair-sprayed hair. Or because it's about eighty-five degrees in her stuffy kitchen, either. Gram has never had that edge to her voice before. Not with me.

"I couldn't take it anymore," I explain. "Do you have any idea how obsessed she is with weight?"

"Yes, I do." She sets her cigarette in the ashtray and lets it smolder.

"Then how was *I* out of line? You should hear how Libby plays with her bears and dolls. She calls them fat and says she can't eat pretend cake because it'll make her fat."

"And what about you?" She puts both hands on my shoulders. "How obsessed are you?"

"Me? Obsessed? Only because of Mom. Libby and I are by-products of *Mom's* obsession."

"Your mom's not perfect—"

"You can say that again."

"*But* she is a good mom. How has she reacted when you've talked to her about this before last night?" She combs through another chunk and rolls it up tight. The pin digs into my scalp. Gram doesn't leave even a bit of wiggle room. Anywhere.

I flinch. "Um, I haven't talked to her about this before."

She adjusts the pin and it lays flat. "And you chose last night, the night before your aunt's wedding, in front of everyone, to bring it up for the first time? And you don't see anything wrong with that?"

Wisps of smoke curl up from the ashtray. My eyes sting, and a little lump forms in my throat. I think about what I said. About making Libby anorexic. About how being her kid is horrible. About her being a bad mom. In front of everyone. Even people who hardly know us. A scene. That came out of nowhere, for Mom at least. I swallow, but the lump doesn't go away.

"Well, when you put it that way—"

"There are things you don't know." She takes a long drag on her cigarette. I swear the air filters through me. Suffocates me. The tip glows red-hot. *Things I don't know?*

"What things?" The lump pushes against my throat, and sweat trickles down behind my ear.

Gram takes a deep breath and coughs. "You know all that time you spent here when you were little?"

"When Mom was 'finding herself'?" I use finger quotation marks.

"Yeah." Gram combs through a piece of hair and holds it out tight as she leans over to look me in the eye. She is so close that I smell her cigarette-and-coffee breath, see the gold flecks in her hazel eyes. "She was finding herself, all right. Half of her was lost."

I'm desperate to look away. At the cigarette. At the linoleum. At something besides those fiery flecks holding me hostage. Making me sweat. Making me listen. And understand. About my mother.

"What are you talking about?"

"Your dad did a number on her head. When you were a baby, he cheated on her—not with a younger woman, but a woman her age,

237

with two kids just like her. When she asked him why, he told her it was because she'd let herself go."

Let herself go? No way! Suzy Galardi-Logan never lets *anything* go, let alone herself. She is the most in-control person I've never known. Control freak, yes. Someone who would let herself go, no. Never. I think of the picture I found a few weeks ago. Mom was thin—too thin—but still gorgeous and put-together. How could he say that? Dad really *is* a dickhead.

"Really? He said that? No kidding?"

"Fo' shizzle."

I can't help but laugh, even though what she's saying isn't funny at all. She works her way around my head, combing and rolling.

"He knew she cared about how she looked. She always has. But when he started drumming that bullshit into her head, she snapped."

"Snapped?"

"Not like you think. She still took care of you and Tony. She just didn't take care of herself. She refused to eat more than a few bites at a time. And only then to get me and Jackie off her back." She slips a pin in a roller. "She looked like a walking skeleton. She got down to nearly eighty pounds."

I gasp. *Eighty pounds?* Is that even possible?

"Did that hurt?" She removes the pin.

"No," I say. "That's fine. It's just—eighty pounds? Really?"

"Really." More coffee-and-cigarette breath. "She was sick. It was horrible."

Oh my God. The lump in my throat feels like it's going to choke me, and tears puddle in my eyes. "I have a picture," I say. "Of you and me—"

Gram walks into her bedroom and returns with a picture. "This?"

"Yeah! That's the one." Why does she have it, too?

"She needed help," Gram continues with the story and the comb, "so Jackie convinced her to check herself into a hospital where she could get it. And insisted on this picture. She hoped it'd help your mom see what she looked like. And remind her of all she had to fight for."

Aunt Jackie. Tells it like it is and doesn't let anyone off the hook.

"Did it work?"

"Eventually. When she came home, she was fifteen pounds heavier and looked closer to herself than she had in years. She still had a ways to go to get healthy, but we took what we could get."

"And then she found Mike and lived happily ever after?"

"I suppose—eventually—but it wasn't that easy."

"Is there more?"

She unplugs the rollers and puts out her cigarette. "There's always more. Remember that. Nobody's story can be summed up over a head of rollers and a couple cigarettes. People are complicated, so don't be so hasty when judging."

Judging? I never thought about *me* judging. Only about how people judge me. I purse my lips and nod. Then I wonder why Gram brought me home with her. Did Mom ask her to? Is Mom so mad that she doesn't want me at her house anymore? They sent Tony to Dad's. Are they sending me to Gram's? Like when Mom was sick? Is that why Gram is telling me all this, not Mom?

"What's the matter with you?" Gram asks. "You look like your puppy died."

"Did Mom kick me out? Am I here to *live* with you?"

"What the—? Whatever gave you that idea?" Gram pulls me to my feet, wraps her arms around me, and squeezes. Then she holds me at arm's length and looks at me. "Your mom was pretty shook up after everything you said, and I thought you both could use a breather. Besides, I wanted to talk to you. It was my idea, and nobody tells me that I can't have my Antoinette overnight if I want her. But there's no way your mom would let me keep you."

"You sure?"

"Of course I am." She swats my behind and says, "We better get a move on if we're going to get to the park on time. Jackie'll kill me if we're late."

She finishes my hair and when I look at it, I'm stunned. It is not how I would ever do it in a million years, but it's kind of cool. She has pulled up most of the curls into a messy bun; a few trail down my neck. I think she must have used a thousand bobby pins. She helps with my makeup, too, so I'm wearing more than usual. I like it, though. The hair, makeup—and, of course, glitter—add a bit of glamor that I'm not used to.

Gram looks beautiful. Her hair is perfectly coiffed, and she has sparkly butterfly combs poking out of it. Her dress is iridescent and flowy and sheer, so I'm not sure what color it is, but I think it might be light green.

And through it all, I think. A lot. All this time, I've been focusing on how messed up I am and blaming Mom—never once cutting her any slack. I criticized her because I thought she was anal and perfect, and expected me to be, too. But, really, she's just like me: *im*perfect—and not exactly as she looks from the outside. I feel guilty, which is a feeling I am very familiar with, but instead of stuffing my face like I used to, I think I'll find Mom and talk to her. Find out if she's okay. Find out for myself if she's mad enough to kick me out. Find out if she'll accept an apology.

46

WHEN WE GET TO THE PARK, I FIND MOM SUPER-
vising Chris's brother-in-law and Mike setting up the chairs
under the pavilion. "There needs to be an aisle!"

How does she glide in her heels like that? Even though I prac-
ticed, I have to focus just to stay upright. She is gorgeous, as usual.
Actually, not as usual. Better than usual. I think my knowing that
she isn't perfect makes her even prettier. Her dress is flawless—
sleek and sexy. Raynee did an amazing job tailoring the skirt.

Libby's dress is pale yellow, and her hair is in a bun with curls
framing her face. "I'm Belle from *Beauty and the Beast*," she
says, twirling. "And I'm wearing hair spray and lipstick, too." She
smacks her lips together.

"Pretty, Lib." I hug her and send her off to run with Judd, who's
decked out in a suit. "Mom?" I ask quietly from outside the pavilion. "Can I talk to you?"

"Sure." She stops what she's doing and comes over to me.

I start to cry. I can't help it. I don't even feel it coming on. The
tears just come out of nowhere. Good thing I'm wearing water-

proof mascara. I pat down my dress, as if that will suddenly make a pocket containing a Kleenex appear. Mom yanks one out of her cleavage and hands it to me. I go from crying to laughing.

"You stuffed the front of your dress with Kleenex?"

"My only sister is getting married." She smiles. "I come prepared."

"Thanks," I say, "And I'm sorry. I mean it. I'm really sorry."

"Me, too." Her hand runs across the pavilion railing.

"What are *you* sorry for?"

"I didn't know I was messing you and Libby up so much." She picks at some loose paint.

I'm not sure what to say next. There's still a lot I don't understand. We stand there awkwardly for a while, both fidgeting. Her with the paint, me with my nails.

"Gram told me some stuff about when I was little," I say finally.

"Oh?" Still looking at the railing.

At the same time, Mom and I start. I say, "I didn't—" and she says, "What—" Then she says, "Sorry. What were you going to say?"

I say, "Nothing. You go."

But neither of us does. I watch Judd chase Libby in circles. Mom nibbles on the inside of her cheek.

"Libby looks adorable in her dress," I say.

"She looks just like you did."

"Yeah?"

"Yeah."

"Mom?"

"Hmm?"

"Why didn't you tell me?" I ask. "You know, about when you were sick?"

"It's not something I'm proud of." She goes back to picking at the paint.

"You couldn't help it."

"Maybe not, but . . ." She looks around the park like she's looking for a reason to bolt from this conversation. The florist arrives and unloads baskets of flowers from her van.

"I've done the best I could," she finally says. "Do you have any idea how it feels to white-knuckle it through every meal? Knowing you have to eat something but terrified of every bite?"

"I know about white-knuckling, yes." Never, never, never has it ever occurred to me that it takes effort for someone to eat. I've spent so much time trying *not* to.

"Believe it or not, I thought that keeping food in the house and letting you guys eat whenever you want would make you not be like me." She pulls another Kleenex out of her dress and blows her nose. "I didn't want you to be obsessed with food. I really didn't realize . . . Not until last night."

"I'm sorry. I really am." I lean on the railing. "I should have talked to you a long time ago. Like when I heard Libby tell her toys how to not be fat. And when I realized how she notices everything we do, say, and eat—or don't eat. I shouldn't have bottled it up and let it explode all over Aunt Jackie's rehearsal dinner." Tears drop one by one down Mom's cheek. "I just didn't think you'd understand. I thought you were perfect."

Mom half-laughs. "Perfect? How can I be perfect and mess you up at the same time?"

"That's the beauty of screwed-up thinking. It doesn't make sense."

"Believe me, I understand more than you think."

I take a deep breath, not sure what to say. Mom understanding is a new concept that's going to take time to adjust to.

"Come on, you two," Gram yells across the pavilion to us. "The wedding is about to start."

When we get over to where the flowers and chairs are set up, Gram says, "Don't you two look like the cat's pajamas!"

On cue, Mom and I both say, "Just the look we were going for."

47

THE CEREMONY IS BEAUTIFUL. I'VE NEVER SEEN
Aunt Jackie so happy. She and Chris both wear white pantsuits.
Jackie's is brocaded with pearls on the fitted sleeveless jacket. She
says she's never liked dresses, and today is no exception.

First Mom walks with one of Chris's sisters, and I walk with the
other. We all carry bouquets of assorted white flowers accented
with salmon-colored ribbon.

Then the twins. Libby has a basket of white flower petals. She
walks slowly and deliberately, and drops a single petal for each
step. She looks so serious. Judd has a sly smile on his face like he's
up to something. I half expect him to throw the ring pillow or
start dancing, but he doesn't. Finally Aunt Jackie and Chris walk
down the aisle. Together.

Once we're all in place, the ceremony begins. The minister
speaks, and then a friend of theirs recites a poem. Aunt Jackie
and Chris wrote their own vows. Chris's are traditional and senti-
mental; she uses words like *cherish our union* and *nurturing love*.
I don't hear it all because I am distracted by Judd poking Uncle

Doug. They're sitting in the front row with Libby, Tayla, Mike, and Gram. I can't look at Gram because she keeps making faces at me, and I don't want to laugh inappropriately.

Aunt Jackie's vows are like none I've ever heard before. Instead of *in sickness and in health*, she promises *to cook soup whenever Chris is sick* and *to always go to Pilates*. Instead of *for richer and poorer*, she vows *to balance the checkbook* monthly, *not annually*, and *to stay away from the Shopping Channel*—after *the food dehydrator arrives*. Chris tears up, as if Aunt Jackie had written a sonnet. Mom laughs and cries at the same time. Some people say, "Awww," and others laugh. Even with a few light moments, the ceremony is sincere and heartfelt.

Before I know it, Jackie and Chris are walking back down the aisle. Everyone is smiling and cheering. I'm glad to be part of it, whether I lost the weight or not. I have Aunt Jackie to thank. She wouldn't let me back out, just like she wouldn't let Mom waste away.

The photographer needs to take about a thousand pictures, so as the other guests leave the pavilion, the family has to wait. Someone lingers in the back. The sun is in my eyes, so it takes a minute for me to realize who it is. Tony!

I hurry over to him, trying not to break my ankle in these stupid heels, and hug him. I'd forgotten how tall he is. He squeezes me tight. Then I swat his arm. "Where have you been?"

"School." He laughs nervously. Almost shy. So not like Tony. "You look . . . wow!"

"Thanks." I want to say something light and clever and funny. I want to laugh. I want everything to be okay. But I have so many questions, and I don't know where to start. And today isn't a good day to get into it all, anyway. So instead I stand there trying to keep my lip from quivering.

Tony notices—he always notices—and hugs me again. This time he doesn't let go. "I'm sorry," he whispers into my hair. "I've been such a dickhead."

I laugh out loud. He looks at me, confused.

"Sorry. It's just that . . . that word reminds me of . . . Dad."

Then it's his turn to crack up. "Yeah, that about sums him up."

By now, everyone else notices Tony, and he's smothered in hugs. The twins don't remember him, so they hide behind Mom.

The photographer calls Aunt Jackie for some shots of her with Chris's family. She tells us to gather because she'll be ready for us soon. As Mom and Mike round up the twins and Gram hunts down Uncle Doug and Tayla, Tony says to me, "So what was up with that picture on Facebook?"

Oh, shit. "You saw that?"

"*You* dancing. With a red Solo cup? Sure did." His face looks like it always has: sharp, bony, intense.

"Uh, I . . . um . . ." Where do I start? There's so much to tell.

"Don't worry," he says. "I took care of it."

"You?" It disappeared because of Tony? "How?"

"Ann!" Mom yells. "Come on. We need you." She grabs hold of Judd, who's pulling away. His attention span has reached its limit.

I wait for Tony to finish. I really want to know.

"I taught the punk kid who posted it some skateboard tricks a while back. He owed me."

Somehow I bet there's more to it. With Tony, there always is. But I don't ask. He kisses my cheek, and I hurry to take my place next to Mom.

Aunt Jackie says she wants Tony in the pictures, too, but when we look for him, he's gone. Slipped out when nobody was watching. But we find a card on a chair. Aunt Jackie opens it right away. Inside are an Olive Garden gift card and a note. She reads, "Dear Aunt Jacks and Chris, Congratulations! Enjoy your day. I'll be back soon. Love, Tony."

Gram puts her arm around Mom, who's crying and dabbing her eyes with a tissue.

They whisper to each other and then both start laughing.

"What?" asks Aunt Jackie.

Gram says, "I asked her if she needed more tissues, and she said, 'I hope not. There's practically a whole box stuffed under my boobs.'"

When we get to the reception hall, I'm surprised by how many people are there—at least two hundred. They must have invited everyone they know.

Raynee has already arrived. "You look amazing!" she says.

"Thanks."

"Where did you get that dress?" she teases.

"It's custom." I twirl around. "Part Snapz! and part Raynee Gilbert."

"Stunning!"

"Thank you." I hug her. "For everything."

The caterers are nearly set up for dinner. Then I notice two familiar faces lighting the Sterno under the chafing dishes. Courtney. And Jon.

My heart starts doing the Thriller. At first I'm not sure if it's because of Courtney or Jon. Courtney has a track record of ruining parties. But since my gaze is stuck on Jon, I'm willing to bet he's the reason. He is so cute in his black dress pants and pressed button-down white shirt. It's tucked in and kind of tight, so his ripped arms and little pouchy belly show through. *Don't stare. Look nonchalant.* Like usual, I can't listen to myself. I gawk unabashedly. I can't help it.

Raynee must have noticed at the same time I do. "Look at that," she says.

"What are they doing here?" Not even glancing away from Jon for a second.

"I guess your aunt hired Jon and Courtney's aunt Joan," says Raynee.

Way to go, Aunt Jackie! Thanks for helping me with my love life!

"She *is* an amazing caterer," says Raynee. "Her food is really good; she's booked practically every weekend. Makes sense that Courtney would get a job with her, I guess."

"As long as she doesn't steal the food." We crack up.

Mom waves me over to the head table, so I take my seat. I pretend to give my full attention to Chris's sister's toast, but my mind is still wrapped around Jon. Is he just like his cousin? A phony? Have they talked about me behind my back? Or maybe Jon hasn't talked about me at all. Or thought about me. After all, he hasn't called. I go out of my way not to look in the direction of the buffet.

For Mom's toast, she starts out with a story about how some girls get dolls to dress up, but she had a real live baby sister to play with. Then she says that when Jackie was in high school, Mom tried setting her up with this really nice guy from down the street. "I just couldn't figure out why she wasn't interested," says Mom. Everyone laughs. "But now, seeing her so happy, I couldn't imagine anyone else for her but Chris. Welcome to the family, Chris!" Mom gets a resounding, "Awww," for that.

"If only Dad were here," she continues. Then from under the table she pulls a framed picture of Gramps and sets it on the table. Another laugh. "Jackie, you know what he'd say?" Jackie watches, waiting. Mom looks to Uncle Doug, who clearly has a line here but has spaced out. Mom repeats, louder, "You know what Dad would say if he were here?"

Uncle Doug stands, and yells, "What? No bacon?" The whole room erupts.

"Seriously, Jack," Mom raises her glass. "Dad would be so proud of you. We all are! Please raise your glasses, everyone, and join me in toasting my sister and her beautiful bride. Cheers!" Applause and clinking glasses. Aunt Jackie and Chris both hug Mom, and so do I.

Then we all go through the line. I avoid Courtney, who's by the doorway to the kitchen. I try not to listen, try not to look at her. I feel her watching, though. What is there about just seeing her that makes me feel like I don't deserve to be here? Or anywhere.

But I *do* belong here. It's *my* aunt's wedding. Not the stupid Knee party. I am a bridesmaid. And while I might not look like the prom queen yet, I'm rocking this dress—a Snapz! dress, no less. Found and altered by her ex-friend—*my* new friend! My hair and makeup are fierce. And after hours of practice, I've even mastered walking in my strappy heels. Courtney can smirk all she wants. She's the one standing against the wall in a hairnet.

As I near her, I suck in a deep breath and hold it. As much as I'd love to make a snide comment, I know I never would. But I will glide past her. I will not cower. She slips into the kitchen just before I get within speaking distance.

She backed down. I didn't.

I don't see Jon at first. But as I'm leaving the food tables, he cuts between Chris's mom and Mike to replace the nearly empty green bean dish. I watch his eyes scan the line and land on me. Once they do, I look down and away. Like I didn't see him. I turn and walk to the table, not caring one bit who is watching and who isn't.

Libby sits between Mom and me at the head table, but Judd insists on sitting at the family table with Gram, Mike, Doug and Tayla, and Raynee. Mom and I talk about the wedding and how beautiful Jackie and Chris are. Nobody mentions fat or fattening, and I don't even think about seconds.

Partly because the food line snakes around the whole room. Partly because Jon and Courtney hover around the buffet. But most of all, because I'm excited about eating a normal meal like a normal person—not a person on a diet or a person eating like there's no tomorrow. A person who can eat and enjoy and stop.

I notice that Mom eats, too. Maybe not everything, but she eats. Libby does, too.

Chris and Jackie cut the cake and everyone cheers when they feed it to each other.

Then Chris's nieces bring plates around to everyone. They bring mine, Mom's, and Libby's at the same time.

I take a bite. "It's really good." Actually it's better than really good. I haven't eaten cake practically all summer. Not since the strawberry shortcake Mom made when Regina visited.

252

"Is it?" Mom picks up a fork, pokes it into her cake, and hesitates. I hold my breath. Then she takes a bite. "Mmmm."

I wonder how long it's really been since Mom's eaten a piece of cake. I wonder if she even knows. Libby takes a bite, too. It might be just a piece of cake, but all of us eating together feels better than anything I've felt in a long time.

48

BOTH BRIDES THROW THEIR BOUQUETS AT THE same time. Jackie blows me a kiss before she turns around, so I know she's aiming for me. I catch it, no problem. Tayla dives to catch Chris's. Everyone claps, and I blush as I go back to my seat.

When the DJ starts the music, I abandon the head table and sit with Raynee. The first dance is Chris and Jackie's. Raynee and I watch Jon and Courtney clean up without actually watching them.

"Has Courtney talked to you?" I ask.

"No. She pretty much hates me now."

"I'm sorry. It's all my fault."

"No, it's not. It's hers." Then Raynee seems to suddenly remember something. "Hey, I meant to tell you earlier, but your mom called you to the table before I could." She leans in. "I talked to Melanie this morning. She says Jon was in Florida because his grandfather fell."

"Oh, no!" I say. "Is he okay?"

"I think so, but I guess they're moving him back to Michigan.

Jon and his parents have been down there the past two weeks, packing up and stuff. Maybe that's why he hasn't called?"

I don't tell Raynee, but I doubt it. I feel bad about his grandpa, and I'm sure his family has had a lot going on. But who am I? I'm just a girl who served him a pretzel, bought a pair of sneakers from him, and puked on his. Even Disney can't spin that into a romance.

The next dance is the bridal party. The music starts—"We Are Family" by Sister Sledge. Mom and Jackie and Chris and Lisa and Carrie all run out and start grooving. Aunt Jackie catches my eye and beckons me onto the dance floor. I pretend I don't see her.

Part of me wants to go out there. Aches to go out there.

I look over to the buffet tables. Courtney is watching me. Then her aunt—at least I assume it's her aunt—wheels a cart over and says something, and she wheels it out of the room. I hate that she still makes me feel self-conscious.

Raynee and I watch the dance floor and smile. Gram is getting down. Shaking it, dancing, singing. I'd love to be like her. Libby and Judd are out there showing off their adorable moves.

"Hey." Suddenly standing behind my shoulder is Jon.

"Hey," I say.

Raynee gets up and grabs her glass. "I'm going to get a refill. Want one?"

"Sure," I say.

"How's it going?" Jon sits in Raynee's seat. "Haven't seen you since . . ."

"Yeah," I watch the dance floor and don't actually make eye contact. "Since. How are your shoes?"

A slow song starts. "They're fine." He laughs. "So did Raynee tell you that I asked for your number?"

"Yeah." I fold and fold and fold a napkin left on the table. I can't look at him. Those dimples. Those eyes.

"I'm sorry I haven't called yet," he said. "I've, um . . . I've wanted to. It's just that . . . um . . ." I wait. I finally look directly at him. He's blushing. He looks like he did that first day at the Twisted Pretzel. When he said that he wanted to be my first. When he realized what he'd said. And again when he told me he'd asked about me. Awkward. Shy, even.

"It's okay." I pick up a silver confetti heart from the table, crease it down the middle, and bend it back and forth, back and forth. Whether it was because of his grandpa, or because Courtney convinced him not to, or something else—I don't need to hear his explanation. I already know. I know the look. The stammer. The overthinking. I know, because that's how I feel most of the time.

"So . . ." he says.

"How about a dance?" Adrenaline zips through me. Then I realize that Jon didn't say it. Mike puts his hand on my shoulder. "Well, what do you think?"

"Um, I don't know." I look at Jon. "Mike, this is Jon. Jon, this is my stepdad, Mike Logan."

They say hi to each other.

"Go ahead," Jon says. "I'll be here a while. We still have dishes to do and stuff."

"Come on." Mike grins and holds out his hand.

Why does Mike want to dance with *me*? Partly out of curiosity and partly because both Mike and Jon are looking at me expectantly, I get up. At least a slow dance isn't as embarrassing as a fast one.

I put one hand on Mike's shoulder and take his other in my hand. He leads me step, step, step around the dance floor. He's actually pretty good, so he makes me feel like less of a klutz. "You look pretty today, Ann," he says so sweet and serious that I feel my face get hot and my nose tingle, like it does just before I cry. As we sway, I try to think if Mike's ever said anything like that to me before. Part of me thinks he has, but I can't remember when.

Five words. Five nice words from a man—a fatherly figure. Words that dads say to daughters, but not mine.

"Thanks, Mike," I say. And I mean it.

"I'm proud of how hard you've worked," he says quietly. "I've wanted to say it for a while, but when it comes to you ladies and your diets, I never know if I'm going to offend."

Mike noticed? And he's *proud*? I giggle a little bit. I'm sure it is a little tricky living with Mom and me and our weight roller coasters.

"So, who's that guy Jon?" he asks.

Why does he want to know? "He's just a guy I know."

"Just checking." He twirls me around. "He likes you."

My heart twirls faster than I do. "What do you mean? How do you know?"

"I'm a guy, Ann." He looks right at me and raises his eyebrows. "I know."

I feel a smile spread across my face. I suppress it and try to look nonchalant.

"Is he a good guy?" he asks.

"Yeah, I think so. Why?"

The music stops. Mike keeps hold of my hand. "Just checking. Gotta keep tabs on the guys who are dealing on my daughter." Then he leans down and kisses my forehead. "Thanks for the dance." He walks away. Back to the head table with Mom.

He called me his daughter. Not his stepdaughter, but his daughter. I completely surrender to the smile.

49

BEFORE I GET BACK TO MY SEAT, THE NEXT SONG
starts. "Thriller." Aunt Jackie squeals and grabs Chris's hand.
Mom, Gram, Chris's sisters, and Tayla line up. Lots of others flock
to the dance floor, too. Their heads and hands jerk in time to the
rhythm.

Libby runs over to me. "Come on, Ann. They're playing our
song." She takes my hand and drags me.

They're playing our song? Where does she get this stuff?

I'm already on the dance floor. Mom and Aunt Jackie get out of
line and help Libby drag me to the front with them. Mom waves
Raynee up with us, too.

"You're dancing with us, kiddo, like it or not," Aunt Jackie yells
above the blaring music. "It's my wedding day, and I want my
whole family dancing with me!"

I don't have time to think, to weigh my options, to decide. I go
where I'm pulled, and I start moving. I step in time with everyone
else.

I'm dancing. Dancing like no one is watching. Even though I

know they are. I know Courtney is against the wall behind the buffet table, watching, judging, laughing. Jon is in the sea of strangers, who are all watching, too. Watching the jiggle.

But as the music continues and I have to concentrate on each step to keep up and not trip over people, I get into it.

I forget that I'm self-conscious, even in front of my own mother. My mother, who I never thought got it. But now I know she gets more than I imagined.

I forget about not fitting. A Snapz! size three zips all the way up. And my friend couldn't care less if it did. And while the shape of my family might not match other families—or even what I imagined it should be—some pretty amazing people make room for me, watch out for me, and love me. Sometimes, even when I don't know it. Make it so I fit. No matter what.

After the second verse, I forget about myself completely.

I let go. And I like it.

50

WHEN "THRILLER" IS OVER, RAYNEE AND I HEAD
back to the table. Jon isn't there. Raynee must have noticed me
looking because she says, "He had to help his aunt load her van. I
think he's coming back."

She's right. Half an hour later, at the beginning of another slow
song, he walks right over and says, "Want to dance?"

Three words. My heart and my stomach switch places for a
second.

*Don't scream. Don't giggle. Just get up. Get up. He'll know that
means yes. Get up.*

I do, and we walk to the dance floor. I don't dance with him the
same way I dance with Mike. Instead I put both hands around his
neck, and he puts both of his around my waist. He doesn't lead
me around the floor like Mike does, either. We pretty much stand
in one place and sway a little. I don't care. I can feel the warmth
of his hand through my dress. Even though it's about a thousand
degrees in this room and I've been dancing—and sweating—I
refuse to pull away. I refuse to think about Courtney watching.

I hope she's watching. And fuming. I'm dancing with her cousin. Her cute cousin.

Jon.

The guy who ate my first crummy pretzel. And then asked who I was. The guy with the most amazing dimples. The guy whose shoes I hurled on, but he still asked Raynee for my number. The guy who asked me to dance.

"You did better at 'Thriller' tonight than you did on the Fourth."

"Gee, thanks." I adjust the scarf strap on my dress. "Don't worry, I haven't been drinking tonight. Your shoes are safe."

"Good to know." He steps on my foot. It kills, but I tell him it doesn't hurt at all.

"In fact, I don't ordinarily drink."

"I know. Raynee told me."

"Cool." That was lame. *Come up with something better than that, quick.*

Before I can think of anything—which would probably take days, maybe even weeks, anyway—a wedding slide show starts on the wall. Everyone stops what they're doing and watches. Jon and I stop dancing, too, but he keeps one of his arms around my waist. I don't pull away. I'm not sure what to do with my arm, though. It feels weird draped around his shoulders. I let it fall a little down his back. It's wet. He's sweating, too.

I don't want to pull away from Jon, so with my other arm, I motion for Raynee to join us. She drags some chairs over. I don't want to sit down because then Jon's arm will move, but we do, and I'm right, his arm moves.

The pictures are beautiful. The flowers and the natural light-ing make the wedding in the park look like a fairy tale. There's one of Mom, Chris's sisters, and me walking down the aisle.

"There you are." Jon nudges me with his arm, then he leaves it on the back of my chair. I lean into it. I look from the screen to his face watching the screen. He's smiling, dimples and all. I'd love to know what he's thinking.

There are pictures of the ceremony—Jackie and Chris giving their vows. They're great together. Who cares what people like Regina think? Another of the twins looking bored. And Gram making a face—the photographer caught her. Now I *can* laugh. Oh, and there's one of Tony and me hugging! "That's my brother," I tell Jon. I make a mental note to get a copy.

Pictures of the families come next.

There I am again. Aunt Jackie and Chris are in the middle and Mom and I are on either side of them. Gram is next to me. Mike is next to Mom. Doug is next to Gram with Tayla on the end, kind of in front of him. The twins stand in front of Mom and me. *My fam-ily.* Most of it, anyway. I remember Tony's note to Aunt Jackie—*I'll be back soon*—and I hope it's true.

There's another picture of me, Mom, and Libby eating cake. I have a mouthful, which is super embarrassing. But the part that I notice even more is Mom. Her mouth is full, too, which is a rare sight, but she's watching me, not the camera, and her eyes are sparkling. She's smiling—a weird, mouth-full-of-cake smile, but a smile nonetheless.

She looks proud. She's watching me like she's proud.

Mom's sitting with Mike, each of them with a twin on their

laps. She notices me and winks. Then pictures of "Thriller" flash up there, and everyone laughs. Not a mean laugh, but in fun. I laugh, too.

I've always hated looking at pictures of me. Still do, really. For some reason, they show fat even more clearly than a mirror does. I'm still not at my ideal weight. I didn't lose forty-five pounds before the wedding. Who knows if I ever will. I've lost twenty-seven and a half pounds, and that's better than nothing. Somehow, though, today I'm thinking more about what I've gained than what I've lost.

ACKNOWLEDGMENTS

Colossal, heartfelt thanks:

To my dream agent, Sara Crowe, for taking a chance on me. To my brilliant editor, Sharyn November, for "getting" my vision for this story and for knowing exactly what it needed. To the Viking team, for caring enough to make *45 Pounds (More or Less)* one of your own.

To the Vermont College of Fine Arts community, especially my fellow workshoppers, for your support, suggestions, and enthusiasm. To my accomplished advisors, especially Martine Leavitt and Rita Williams-Garcia, for challenging me and for going above and beyond. To my beloved Bat Poets, especially Cori McCarthy and Kate Hosford, for your impeccable sonar, ability to hang upside down, and propensity to flight. Your generosity astounds me.

To my critique group, the Feathered Pens—Barb Etlin, Susan See, and Cana Rensberger—for not laughing at those horrible early drafts. To the Lucky 13s and the Class of 2k13, for your camaraderie. You rock!

To my amazing friends, Pat Gallagher, Barb Garner, Brenda Sas, and Sheila Wald, for braving that blizzard and for toasting every celebration. To Vicky Lorencen, for introducing me to SCBWI and for encouraging me to take those first steps. I don't deserve any of you.

Most of all, to my family—Larry, Alex & Paige, Max, Nicole, & Madalyn, Sylvia, Avery, Brandon, & Iris—for putting up with me. To Dad and Mom, for always believing that I could do anything, even when I wasn't sure. I love you!

To you, the reader, for picking up this book. I hope you like it.

K. A. Barson earned an MFA in Writing for Children and Young Adults from Vermont College of Fine Arts. She and her husband live in Jackson, Michigan, surrounded by kids, grandkids, unruly dogs, and too many pairs of shoes. This is her first novel.

Visit her website at www.kabarson.com.